Magic Kitten

A Summer Spell

Magic Kitten
Duos

A Summer Spell
& Classroom Chaos

SUE BENTLEY

Illustrated by Angela Swan

PUFFIN

Bradley — my lovely laid-back blue boy
Brian — the shy blue twin

PUFFIN BOOKS

Published by the Penguin Group
Penguin Books Ltd, 80 Strand, London WC2R 0RL, England
Penguin Group (USA) Inc., 375 Hudson Street, New York, New York 10014, USA
Penguin Group (Canada), 90 Eglinton Avenue East, Suite 700, Toronto, Ontario, Canada M4P 2Y3
(a division of Pearson Penguin Canada Inc.)
Penguin Ireland, 25 St Stephen's Green, Dublin 2, Ireland (a division of Penguin Books Ltd)
Penguin Group (Australia), 250 Camberwell Road, Camberwell, Victoria 3124, Australia
(a division of Pearson Australia Group Pty Ltd)
Penguin Books India Pvt Ltd, 11 Community Centre,
Panchsheel Park, New Delhi – 110 017, India
Penguin Group (NZ), 67 Apollo Drive, Rosedale, North Shore 0632, New Zealand
(a division of Pearson New Zealand Ltd)
Penguin Books (South Africa) (Pty) Ltd, 24 Sturdee Avenue, Rosebank,
Johannesburg 2196, South Africa

Penguin Books Ltd, Registered Offices: 80 Strand, London WC2R 0RL, England

puffinbooks.com

Summer Spell first published 2006
Classroom Chaos first published 2006
First published in one volume 2008

2

Text copyright © Sue Bentley, 2006
Illustrations copyright © Angela Swan, 2006
All rights reserved

The moral right of the author and illustrator has been asserted

Set in Bembo
Typeset by Palimpsest Book Production Limited, Grangemouth, Stirlingshire
Made and printed in England by Clays Ltd, St Ives plc

British Library Cataloguing in Publication Data
A CIP catalogue record for this book is available from the British Library

ISBN: 978-0-141-32448-7

www.greenpenguin.co.uk

Penguin Books is committed to a sustainable future
for our business, our readers and our planet.
The book in your hands is made from paper
certified by the Forest Stewardship Council.

Prologue

There was a flash of bright white light and a shower of silver sparkles. Where the young white lion had stood, now crouched a tiny, fluffy, marmalade kitten. Overhead, grey clouds skidded across a huge red moon.

Suddenly an old grey lion ran up to the little kitten and bowed his head. 'Prince Flame! Hurry! Your Uncle

Ebony comes! If he finds you, he will kill you. You must use this disguise and hide until your powers grow stronger.'

'Cirrus! Save yourself,' Flame mewed, his emerald eyes flashing. 'I will face him.'

'Please, Flame. You must hide,' Cirrus urged.

Flame shivered. 'Hide where? My kingdom is taken. Uncle's spies are everywhere . . .'

Cirrus laid a paw on the young prince's little marmalade head. 'Go far away. Grow strong and wise. Return then, to claim the Lion Throne and rid the land from this terrible evil.'

Something moved on the lower slopes. Flame gasped as an enormous adult lion surged upwards in great, muscular bounds that ate up the wet grass. His terrifying teeth were bared.

Silver sparks ignited in Flame's fur and the kitten mewed as he felt the power building inside him.

Just as the older lion leapt on to a flat rock and gathered himself for a final spring, there was a bright blue flash. Flame heard a roar of rage, then felt himself falling. Falling . . .

Chapter
★ ONE ★

Lisa Morgan gave a sigh as the train drew to a halt. Long Brackby station had no waiting room. There was just a wooden platform and some steps that led down to the road. All around there was miles of open countryside.

'Great, I'm being dumped in the middle of nowhere,' she grumbled. 'Thanks a lot, Mum and Dad!'

Her parents had gone to America on business. But Lisa was going to stay with her Aunt Rose, who she hadn't seen since she was a baby.

Lisa scanned the platform. She saw a woman with plaits and flowing clothes hurrying towards her. Her heart sank. Aunt Rose was an old hippie!

I bet she has weird ideas about food, Lisa thought glumly. She imagined being force-fed beans, lettuce and raw carrots. She pictured herself looking all limp and pale. Wouldn't that just serve her parents right?

The hippie woman smiled. She dashed straight past Lisa and jumped on the train.

'Phew!' Lisa breathed, feeling relieved but a bit disappointed. She had quite liked the idea of making her parents feel guilty for not taking her with them.

Just then a voice called out, 'Hi, Lisa! I'm over here!'

A slim woman with wavy brown hair was climbing the platform steps. She wore jeans and a yellow T-shirt. She waved at Lisa.

Lisa waved back.

'Sorry I'm a bit late.' Rose gathered Lisa up and gave her a big hug. She then held Lisa at arm's length and studied her. 'Gosh, aren't you tall for ten years old?'

'Everyone says that,' Lisa murmured. 'Dad says I take after him.'

'I expect you're right.' Rose's smile was warm. It made her eyes twinkle. 'It's so lovely to have you for the school holidays. We can really get to know each other.'

Lisa felt cheered by Rose's warm welcome. But she wasn't ready to let go of her bad mood. 'I didn't want to come here. Mum forced me to stay with you.'

Rose looked amused. She picked up

Lisa's suitcase. 'Well – I'd better make sure you enjoy yourself then. Long Brackby may not compare with America, but it has a lot to offer. Come on. Let's go home. The car's this way.'

Lisa followed her aunt down the steps. The car park was empty. 'Has someone stolen your car?' she asked worriedly.

'Oh, no. Matilda's over there.' Rose pointed across a wide field. 'She conked out on me, I'm afraid. That's why I was late.'

Lisa craned her neck. She could just see the rounded top of a red car above a hedge. It looked about a hundred miles away!

Rose grinned at Lisa's expression. 'It's

only a short walk. I expect you could do with stretching your legs after two hours on the train.' She opened a big wooden gate and stepped into the field.

Lisa hung back nervously. There were lots of enormous black and white cows in the field. 'Won't they chase us?' she asked.

'Not if we don't chase them,' Rose joked. 'Just follow me. You'll be fine.' She closed the gate behind them and set off.

After a couple of metres Rose stopped suddenly. 'Oh, look, how pretty. That's ragged robin . . .' She pointed to a clump of pink wild flowers.

'Oh.' Lisa almost bumped into her aunt. She was keeping a wary eye on the cows. One of them, which looked about the size of a bus, was staring hard at her. She was sure it was going to charge at any moment. Rose set off again. 'Lisa, you'd better watch out for the . . .' she began.

Lisa's foot sank right into something soft and smelly. She skidded and almost slipped over. 'Ugh! How gross is that!'

'. . . cowpats,' Rose finished.

'My trainers!' Lisa wailed. 'They're ruined.'

Rose's mouth twitched. 'Oh, well, it's only a bit of old poo. We can hose it off when we get home. Good thing you didn't slip over and sit in it!'

Lisa scowled at Rose. 'Ha, ha,' she muttered crossly.

Peering down at her trainer, Lisa hopped about on one foot, trying to wipe the sole clean on the grass. When she looked up again, she saw that Rose was almost at the other end of the field.

'Wait for me!' she shouted in panic. She zoomed across the field and shot through the gate. There was no way she going to be left behind with the cows, to be trampled into a human pancake!

Rose walked along the grass verge until she came to her car. 'Here we are. Say hello to Matilda.'

Rose's VW Beetle was painted black and tomato red. It looked like a giant, rather battered ladybird.

'Oh – my – goodness,' Lisa mouthed silently. 'Will that old thing start?'

'*She*, please,' Rose corrected, 'Matilda always starts after a rest. She opened the bonnet, which Lisa saw was actually the boot, and put Lisa's suitcase inside. When they were both seated, Rose gunned the engine. 'Hurrah! First time!' she cried.

Despite herself, Lisa smiled.

A couple of minutes later, they drew up outside a neat thatched cottage. White roses scrambled all over the honey-coloured stone walls.

'Leave your trainers on the front step. You can clean them later,' Rose said. 'I expect you'd like a cold drink.'

'Yes, please.' Lisa followed her aunt through to the kitchen. A big iron kettle sat on top of Rose's cooker. There was also a deep sink and a wooden dresser, but no dishwasher, toaster or microwave.

'Now, what can I get you?' asked Rose.

'A Coke, please,' Lisa said.

Rose frowned. 'I'm afraid I've only got lemonade. It's home-made. Would you like to try it?'

Lisa wrinkled her nose, but she was dying of thirst so she accepted a glass. She took a tiny sip. It wasn't as bad as she'd expected.

'Come on. I'll give you the grand tour.' Rose led the way into a room filled with afternoon sunshine.

Lisa saw a sofa with big patchwork cushions and lots of bookcases. 'Through there is my workroom.' Rose pointed towards an open door.

Lisa peered inside. There were shelves piled with folded material, and glass jars crammed with colourful beads and buttons. 'I thought Mum said you were an artist.'

Rose chuckled. 'I'm a textile artist. I make patchwork quilts and wall hangings.'

'Oh,' Lisa said. That sounded really boring. 'What's upstairs?'

Rose explained that there were two bedrooms. One was hers and Lisa would be using the other.

'It's a bit small, isn't it?' Lisa said. She was sure Rose's entire cottage would fit into the sitting room of her parents' flat in London.

'I prefer to think of it as cosy,' said Rose with a smile. 'It suits me just fine. Why don't we sit down and finish our drinks before I show you your room?'

'OK,' Lisa shrugged. She plonked herself down on Rose's squishy sofa.

Something didn't seem quite right with the room. Then, with a shock, she realized why. 'You haven't got a TV!'

'Oh, I don't bother with watching the box. I always have so much to do,' Rose said.

Lisa was speechless. She didn't know *anyone* who didn't have a TV.

Rose took one look at Lisa's glum face. She chuckled. 'I've an old set in the cupboard. I'll get it for you, if you like.'

Lisa shrugged. 'I don't mind.'

Five minutes later Rose came in carrying a small black and white TV. 'Here you go.'

Lisa just stared. 'It's only got four channels!'

Rose frowned. 'How many should it have?'

'I don't know. But ours at home has at least thirty.'

'Really?' Rose looked astonished. 'However do they fill that many channels? Well, if you don't want it . . .'

'No, I do. I do!' Lisa decided quickly.

She watched as Rose set about plugging in the TV. No microwave and a TV that should be in a museum. This holiday was going to be a nightmare.

Chapter
★ TWO ★

As Lisa finished stuffing her clothes into a drawer, her aunt called up the stairs.

'Lisa! Why don't you have a look round outside while I'm cooking supper? There's something that might interest you in the barn.'

Lisa padded downstairs in her socks. Rose was in the kitchen by the back door. She gave Lisa some green wellington boots. 'You can borrow these.'

Lisa rolled her eyes. 'Oh, good!' she murmured.

Rose chuckled. 'They might not be the height of fashion, but they'll keep your feet clean!'

Rose's garden had a long narrow lawn and a big vegetable plot. The old barn was right at the bottom. Lisa wandered down to it. She hoped the barn wasn't dark and creepy and full of horrible spiders.

Just as she opened the door there was a bright silver flash. Lisa thought she saw a large white shape out of the corner of her eye. She turned her head, but saw only a pile of old newspapers.

She pushed the door wide open and
poked her head in. A warm, slightly
musty, smell greeted her. It was
somehow familiar. Lisa went right
inside. She could see rows of cages
and pens. Now she recognized that
smell. It was just like inside a pet
shop.

'Look at all these animals! This is
great!' There were rabbits, guinea pigs

and even some hedgehogs. 'Aunt Rose must be into animal rescue.'

Sacks of animal food were stored on a bench. Lisa noticed a glow coming from one of the food sacks. 'That's strange.' She went over to investigate.

'Oh!' She gazed in amazement.

A fluffy marmalade-coloured kitten was curled up on one of the sacks. Its silky coat looked as soft as thistledown. Silver sparkles glittered in the air around it and its whiskers crackled like electricity.

Lisa stared and stared at the kitten. It looked so real. Was it some kind of new toy? No cat in the world sparkled like that.

Suddenly the kitten's eyes shot open. It took one look at Lisa and hurtled into the air on stiff little legs.

'Miaow! Monster!' it cried fearfully.

'Argh!' Lisa yelled in shock. Did this kitten really just speak?

Lisa took a step back, fell over her own feet and landed on her bottom in the straw.

The kitten gazed at her with glowing emerald eyes. Its fur all stood on end. Silver sparkles crackled all round it. 'What are you?' it demanded in a velvety miaow.

'I'm a girl,' Lisa stammered in complete shock. 'What are you?'

But the kitten didn't seem to hear her. 'A girl?' it repeated to itself. 'Strange. You have two legs. No tail or whiskers.'

'Of course I haven't! I'm not a cat!' Lisa said. She rose to her feet slowly, so that the amazing kitten wouldn't run away. 'My name's Lisa Morgan.'

'Lisa,' the kitten mewed, looking up at her. It seemed strangely unafraid of her, despite how tiny it was. 'Where is this place, Lisa?'

'It's a village called Long Brackby,' she replied. 'My Aunt Rose lives here. I'm staying with her for the holidays. What are you doing here? Who are you? *What* are you?'

'I am Prince Flame,' replied the kitten, sitting up very straight. 'Heir to the Lion Throne.'

'Wow! Really?' Lisa was having trouble taking everything in. A royal cat. A magic, talking cat. Here in her aunt's barn! Lisa thought for a moment. She was confused. 'Did you say *Lion* Throne? But you're only a kit–' She was suddenly interrupted as Flame pricked up his ears.

'What is that big noise?'

Lisa heard a car go by on the road outside. 'Just a car. It's OK. It won't hurt you.' She had a sudden thought. 'Are you hungry? Aunt Rose must have loads of cat food. I can get you some if you like.'

Lisa saw Flame's eyes light up at the
thought of food. 'You are kind, Lisa.
This is a safe place.'

He leapt forward. There was a
bright blue flash and a crackle of silver
sparks.

'Oh!' Lisa was blinded for a second.
When her sight cleared, she saw that in
Flame's place stood a young, regal,
white lion. Then just as suddenly as it

had appeared, Flame returned as the fluffy marmalade kitten.

'Flame? Was that you?' she gasped. 'You really are a lion prince!'

Flame blinked up at her with wide, emerald-green eyes. 'I am in danger. I must hide. Will you keep me safe?' he asked in a tiny mew.

Lisa's heart melted. Flame was impressive as a royal lion. Disguised as a kitten he was adorable. 'Oh, of course I will!' Picking him up, she gently stroked the top of his head. Then she paused for a moment. 'But what are you hiding from?'

Flame placed his tiny paws on Lisa's chest and looked up at her. 'My uncle wants my throne. His spies seek me here. He wants – he wants to kill me.'

'Well, they'll have to fight me first!' Lisa said fiercely. 'I'll look after you, Flame,' she promised. 'You'll be my secret. My secret magic kitten.

Although I don't know what I'm going to tell Aunt Rose. She's going to notice you if you live here.'

'Notice who?' asked a voice at her side. 'Who are you talking to, Lisa?'

Lisa almost jumped out of her skin. She hadn't heard Aunt Rose come into the barn.

Chapter
★ THREE ★

'I found Flame asleep on a feed sack.
Please can I keep him?' Lisa asked,
stroking Flame's tiny ears.

'Flame? I see you've already given
him a name.' Rose stroked the kitten's
soft marmalade fur. 'He's beautiful all
right. But we should find out where he
lives. He's not one of the rescued
animals, you know.'

'He hasn't got a home or he wouldn't
be sleeping in a barn, would he?' Lisa
reasoned. She had promised Flame she
would take care of him and there was *no
way* she was letting him down. 'If you let
Flame live here, I'll do everything for
him. I'll buy his food out of my pocket
money. He can sleep in my bedroom.
And . . . and . . . I'll clean out pongy
animal cages and everything!'

Rose laughed. 'You're determined to keep him, aren't you?'

'Completely!' Lisa said spiritedly. 'So – can he stay?'

'You'd best give him to me then,' Rose said. 'I'll check him for fleas and ticks before he comes into the house.'

'Brilliant! You can stay here. We're going to be the best of friends,' Lisa whispered, giving Flame a swift hug before handing him to her aunt.

'Hello there, you sweet thing.' Rose ran expert fingers through Flame's soft coat. 'No flea dirt showing, so far.' She then turned him over and searched the paler fur on his fat, round tummy. 'Good, none there either.'

Flame wriggled and mewed in protest.

Lisa had to bite back a grin. She suspected this was the first time a lion prince had been searched for fleas!

Rose finished her examination. 'He's clean and in very good condition. I expect he's hungry. You'll find food and a feeding dish on that shelf.'

'Thanks, Aunt Rose! You're wonderful!' Lisa hugged her aunt on impulse.

Rose gave her a pleased smile.
'Anyone would think you'd never had a
pet!'

'I haven't. Mum says it isn't fair to
have animals in a town flat.' Lisa
opened a tin, forked food into a dish
and set it on the floor.

Flame purred loudly as he munched
the cat food.

'Well, I agree with your mum about
pets,' Rose said seriously. 'Don't get too
attached to Flame. You'll have a tough
decision to make when you go back to
London.'

Lisa knew that Rose was right. But it
was too late. She had promised Flame
she would look after him, and this
magic kitten was the one good thing
that had happened since her parents

had left her here. She didn't want to give him up!

Flame licked his lips when he'd finished the food. He came and rubbed his body against Lisa's legs. She bent down to stroke him and he mewed softly, so only she heard him.

'I am safe with you. Thank you, Lisa.'

Rose dug a scoop into a sack of rabbit food. 'Just time to feed this lot before supper.'

'I'll help.' This wasn't exactly Lisa's idea of fun but she was determined to show that she meant to keep her promise and make certain that Flame could stay.

For the next half-hour she refilled

water bottles, chopped vegetables and
replaced soiled straw.

Flame settled down, tucked his paws
beneath his body and dozed.

'Thanks, love,' Rose said later, as she
and Lisa washed their hands. 'I bet
you're ready to eat. I know I am.'

Lisa scooped up the sleepy kitten and
followed Rose back to the cottage.
Rose gave her an old blanket and Lisa
spread it on the sofa. Flame jumped
straight up and began pedalling it into
a soft nest with his front paws.

A few minutes later, Rose brought
heaped plates of food to the table.

'Er . . . thanks.' Lisa poked the food
with her knife. It was shepherd's pie
with a lot of fresh green stuff next to
it.

'That's called salad. We eat a lot in
the country. It's the law!' Rose kept a
straight face.

'I get the message,' Lisa said with a
grin. The pie was delicious and she
even ate some of the salad. Afterwards,
Lisa went to sit near Flame on the
sofa. 'Thanks, Aunt Rose. I think I'll
curl up with Flame and watch TV
now.'

'Do you mind doing that later?' Rose said. 'House rules are – I cook, you wash up. OK?'

'Oh, right.' Lisa felt herself blush. She jumped up and collected the dishes. Wasn't there even a dishwasher here?

In the kitchen, Lisa filled the sink with hot water and squirted washing-up liquid over the pots and pans. As she began scrubbing them clean, suds foamed up past her elbows. 'Oo-er,' she said worriedly, as more suds waterfalled on to the kitchen floor and slopped round her feet. 'I think I overdid it! What a mess. Aunt Rose is going to kill me!'

'May I help?' came a tiny voice from the kitchen floor.

She turned to see that Flame stood

behind her. His marmalade fur was fizzing with huge silver sparkles, his whiskers crackled and his eyes glowed like emerald coals. Lisa felt a hot prickling sensation down her spine.

Something was about to happen!

Chapter
★ FOUR ★

Flame leapt up into the air like a silver
fireball and landed on the draining
board. Sparks crackled from the tips of
his ears.

He waved his front paws and plates,
spoons, forks, knives and pans all
dunked themselves in the suds. One by
one, they jumped into the air and spun
themselves dry.

Lisa's eyes widened. 'This is *so* cool!'

Cupboard doors flew open and
clean plates stacked themselves on the
shelves. Drawers opened, so that forks,
knives and spoons could zoom inside.

Lisa watched the suds drain away.
The dishcloth did a little dance as it
wiped the sink clean. Another cloth
shimmied across the kitchen floor.

'Look at them go!' She clapped her hands with delight.

'Lisa? Are you all right? There's a lot of noise in there,' Rose called from the sitting room.

'Oh, no!' Lisa's hand flew to her mouth. She waved frantically at Flame. 'Quick. Stop doing whatever you're doing!' she hissed. 'I'm fine. Almost finished!' she called to her aunt, in what she hoped was a normal voice.

Crash! Cupboard doors closed. Bang! Drawers slammed shut. Rattle! Cutlery settled into place.

Seconds later, Rose popped her head round the kitchen door. 'What *is* going on out here?'

Flame sat on the floor, looking just like a normal marmalade kitten. Phew! Lisa let out her breath and gave her aunt a rather shaky smile. That was a near thing!

'I'm really impressed. The whole kitchen's spotless. Well done,' Rose said admiringly.

'Oh, it was nothing,' Lisa said, shining the back of her nails on her T-shirt.

She winked at Flame, who gave a mischievous 'miaow'.

A big bubble of laughter lodged in Lisa's chest. With Flame around, she reckoned this holiday might not be so bad after all.

The following morning, Lisa woke early. She lay with her eyes closed, listening for the sound of traffic and taxi horns hooting in impatience. But only birdsong drifted in on the fresh

breeze from the open window. Lisa
opened her eyes as she remembered
where she was.

Aunt Rose's cottage in Long Brackby.
And yesterday she had found a magic
kitten in the barn! He was curled up
asleep in the crook of her arm.

Flame purred softly in his sleep. As
Lisa stroked him gently, Flame stretched

and yawned, showing his little pink tongue and sharp white teeth. Silver sparks glittered in his fur.

'I slept well, thank you,' he purred happily.

'Me too,' Lisa said as Flame rubbed his head under her chin. 'That tickles!' she said with a grin. She pulled herself up out of bed and went in search of the bathroom as Flame made himself comfy on her pillow and waited.

Rose was already in the kitchen when Lisa came down. Lisa fed Flame before she ate her breakfast and then helped Rose clear up, smiling as she remembered how the dishes had got cleaned yesterday!

'Do you fancy cycling to the village store?' Rose asked. 'We need milk,

bread and eggs, but I've got heaps of
sewing to do,' she explained. 'You could
use my bike. It would help me out and
would give you a chance to explore.'

'Sounds great,' Lisa said. Having
Flame along would make even boring
old shopping fun!

Rose fetched her bike. It had a deep

basket on the front. Lisa lined it with
Flame's blanket and then lifted him in.
'There. It's just right for you!'

Flame purred softly in agreement.

Rose laughed. 'You know, I think that
kitten understands every word you say!'

She came round to the front of the
cottage to give Lisa directions to the
village shops. 'Go up Berry Road to
the crossroads and turn right. You'll see
the White Hart Inn. The shops are just
a bit farther on. You can't miss them.'

Rose's red and black VW Beetle was
parked by the gate. 'Hi, Matilda!' Lisa
called as she cycled past. 'See you later,
Aunt Rose!'

The honey scent of hawthorn filled
the lane. Skylarks circled overhead,
drifting on the warm air. Flame had his

nose in the air, sniffing the delicious country smells.

'Now – we turn here,' Lisa reminded herself.

Berry Road was narrow and lined with trees. Lisa began to slow down as she approached a sharp bend.

Suddenly a brown and white pony came hurtling towards her. Lisa caught a glimpse of the rider pulling at the reins. The pony's ears were flat against its head. It snorted loudly, flaring its nostrils.

'Watch out!' shouted the rider. 'I can't stop him!'

Lisa squeezed the brakes hard so that pebbles sprayed the grass verge. Flame dug his claws into the basket to brace himself. But it was too late. They were going to crash!

Chapter
★ FIVE ★

Lisa's bike screeched along the road
into the pony. The brakes locked and
she was launched into the air. Just as
she prepared herself for a very painful
landing there was a silver flash and she
landed softly on to what felt like a very
soft pillow.

'Oh!' she cried in surprise. She
pushed herself shakily to her feet and

looked down, but there was just the
grass verge beneath her. That was a
near thing. Flame must have used
his magic to save her! But where was
he?

Lisa looked round in panic. In the
road she saw the pony was snorting
with pain and fear. His rider was
trying to calm him down. Aunt
Rose's bike lay on its side in the
road, the pedals still going round.
Flame's crumpled blanket was lying
beside it.

Lisa's heart lurched. 'Oh, no!
Flame!'

But Flame was sitting in the gutter,
calmly washing his face. He gave a
pleased little miaow as she bent down
to stroke him.

'Oh, thank goodness you're OK!' Lisa said.

'Yeah? Well, Fly's not. And it's all your fault!' shouted the boy who'd been riding the pony. 'Why don't you look where you're going?'

Stung, Lisa glared at him. The boy looked about twelve. He had dark-brown hair and bright-blue eyes. 'You were on the wrong side of the road!' she protested angrily, picking up her bike.

But the boy ignored her. 'Whoa, there. Calm down, Fly!' he soothed. The pony rolled his eyes and kept lifting one back leg. 'Oh, great. Now he's lame! Dad's going to kill me. We haven't got any money for vets' bills.'

Lisa felt sorry for the pony, but she
was still furious with its owner. 'You
should be more careful how you ride
him then! Look at my aunt's bike. The
front wheel's all buckled!'

Flame finished washing himself. He
padded over to Fly. Lisa started forward
in alarm. Did Flame realize what
danger he was in?

'Get that kitten out of the way. Fly's dead wary of other animals,' the boy warned.

Flame stopped right beneath Fly. He looked straight up at the pony, his emerald eyes sparkling. Fly shifted sideways and gave a nervous blow. Then he dipped his head. Flame purred loudly, closing his eyes with pleasure as Fly snuffled warm breath into his fur.

The boy scratched his head. 'Will you look at that? Fly's really taken to that kitten.' He ran a hand down his pony's sore leg. 'And his leg seems better now. How did that happen?'

Lisa smiled inwardly as she bent down and picked Flame up. 'Thanks for saving me. And making Fly's leg better,' she whispered.

'I am glad to help.' Flame licked her chin with his tiny pink tongue.

Lisa straightened up. 'Oh, well, he can't have been that hurt in the first place,' she said, trying not to laugh at the boy's confusion.

The boy scowled at her. 'Whatever,' he said. 'Come on, Fly. Let's get going.'

'Hey! What about the bike? I can't
ride it like that,' Lisa said with dismay.

'Tough!' The boy grinned cheekily.

Lisa was fuming. She opened her
mouth to reply just as a policeman
came round the corner.

The boy groaned. 'Oh, great. It's
Mike Sanders. He chucked me off the
green for playing football last week.'
He threw a pleading glance at Lisa.
'OK, I *was* on the wrong side of
the road. I couldn't help it. Some
flapping washing startled Fly and he
bolted.'

Lisa folded her arms. 'So?' she said.

The boy hesitated. 'I'll make a
deal with you. You keep quiet about
me and Fly and I'll fix your bent
wheel.'

Lisa grinned. 'Done! I'm Lisa. Lisa Morgan.' She held out her hand. 'And this is Flame.'

'John Wood,' said the boy. He spat in his palm before he shook hands with Lisa, and gave Flame a pat on the head.

The policeman had reached them by now. Mike Sanders had fair curly hair and a pleasant face. He took in the bike with its bent wheel and gave John a stern look. 'Hmm. What have you been up to now?'

John looked down at the road and shuffled his feet. 'Nothing,' he muttered.

Lisa took a step forward. 'It's a good thing John came along,' she said quickly. 'That's my Aunt Rose's bike. The wheel buckled when I fell off. John's offered to mend it for me.'

'Has he?' Mike Sanders looked surprised. 'Good for you, John. That should keep you out of trouble for five minutes.' After checking that Lisa wasn't hurt, he went on his way.

'Phew, that was close,' said John. He took hold of Fly's reins. 'Let's go. I live just over there.'

'Don't say "thanks" for covering for me, will you?' Lisa said.

John laughed. His blue eyes sparkled. 'OK, I won't!'

Lisa couldn't help laughing back. 'Come on, Flame.' She lifted him into the basket and wheeled the bike along in a wobbly line. John walked ahead, leading Fly.

'Down here,' John said, heading down a narrow track that branched off Berry Road.

Brambles, clustered with pink-tinged blossom, rambled through the hedgerows. Peacock butterflies fluttered around clumps of nettles near a fence. Lisa paused for a moment as she looked at a large field filled with caravans beyond an open gate.

John turned round. 'Well, are you coming or what?'

Flame gave a happy miaow. And Lisa pushed him and the wobbly bike through the gate.

Chapter
★ SIX ★

The oldest lady Lisa had ever seen came out of an old-fashioned caravan with fancy carving and red and yellow wheels. She waved at John and beckoned for him to come over.

'That's my great-grandma,' John told Lisa. 'Come and meet her.'

Lisa lifted Flame out of the basket and then laid the bike on its side in the grass. Flame scampered straight up the caravan's sloping wooden steps and began rubbing himself against the old lady's long skirts.

'He's called Flame,' Lisa told her.

John had tied up Fly before climbing the steps. He gave his gran a kiss on her cheek. 'Hi, Gran! All right?'

The old lady's bright eyes crinkled in a smile. 'Fine. Come on inside and bring your new friends. The kettle's on,' she said as she leaned down to stroke Flame. 'I bet you'd like a saucer of milk, wouldn't you?'

Flame mewed eagerly.

Once inside the tiny living space, Lisa glanced round. Shiny pots and pans hung on hooks above a tiny stove, which made the room baking hot.

There was a wonderful smell of
woodsmoke and lavender polish.

Flame lapped at his milk. He seemed
perfectly at home.

John came and sat near his gran.
'Gran, this is Lisa. She's staying with
her aunt in the village. Lisa, meet
Violet Wood – she's head of our
family. Even my dad's a bit afraid of
her. But I reckon her bark's a lot worse
than her bite!'

Violet gave a gap-toothed grin. 'Here!
Don't give away all me secrets!' Round
her shoulders there was a black fringed
shawl with pink roses on it. Big gold
hoops glittered in her ears.

'I like your caravan,' Lisa said politely
as Violet made tea.

'It's me wagon,' Violet corrected. 'A

true Romany don't call their home a caravan.'

'Sorry,' Lisa said.

Violet fixed her with a gaze as bright and shiny as a robin's. 'What you got to be sorry about?'

'Er . . . Nothing,' Lisa murmured.

'No cause to say you're sorry then!' Violet crowed.

John chuckled. 'Stop teasing, Gran. Lisa's all right. She put a word in for me with Mike Sanders.'

Violet poured strong tea into china cups. 'Sanders ain't a bad sort. It's that Robert Higgins you got to watch out for. He's been here again, accusing our men of taking deer. I told him I know everything that goes on round here and there's been no poaching. But he wouldn't have it. He as much as called me a liar to my face!' She sniffed indignantly.

'Who's Robert Higgins?' Lisa asked John.

'Higgins runs the estate for his Lordship,' John explained. 'That bit of forest at the back of your aunt's cottage is part of it.'

'You stay out of his way, John, you hear? He's a nasty piece of work,' Violet warned him.

'Yes, Gran.' John was serious for a moment and then he turned to Lisa. 'Gran used to travel all over the country in this wagon. She's not keen on being here on the official travellers' site.'

'I miss the open road too much.' Violet's beady eyes brightened. 'There was this one time when we was *aitched* up for the night by a river . . .'

'That means camped,' John explained, smiling at Lisa.

Violet told them about the old days, when a pony drew her wagon through the country lanes. 'All the families would meet up with their relatives at horse fairs. There would be dozens of Woods, Smiths, Lees and a hundred other names. Oh, it was grand. In late summer, we'd all travel down to Kent for the hop-picking.'

Lisa listened in fascination. A look of contentment settled on Violet's face as she stroked Flame's soft coat.

Violet saw Lisa watching closely and said, 'Flame's a grand kitten, ain't he?' She closed one eye in a broad wink. 'He's just magic.'

Lisa's eyes widened in shock. *She knows!* she thought. *Violet knows about Flame!*

'Well, Gran. I've got to get my tools to mend Lisa's bike,' John said, apparently not noticing anything. 'Thanks for the tea and stories.'

'You can bring Lisa and Flame to
see me again.' Violet came down the
wagon steps to wave goodbye. She
stood with Lisa as John walked
across to a modern, chrome-trimmed
trailer.

'Keep this special one safe,' Violet
said softly to Lisa as she stroked the top
of Flame's head. 'He'll not be with you
long.'

Lisa gathered Flame in her embrace. She felt a sharp pang at the thought of not having him around. 'I don't want him to leave, ever,' she said, her voice quivering.

Violet's eyes sparkled kindly. She patted Lisa's arm. 'I know. But his destiny is far from here. When the call comes, he must go. Be thankful that he chose you for his special friend.'

Lisa hugged Flame's furry little body close. He purred and licked her chin. She had a lump in her throat. 'I am. If I look after him really well, maybe he'll decide to stay here.'

A wise but sad look crossed Violet's face. 'Maybe,' she murmured.

★

'All finished,' John said, moving the
bike back and forth. 'Good as new!'

He lifted Flame into the basket as
Lisa got on the bike. 'Thanks. Aunt
Rose won't notice a thing. Well – bye
for now,' she said and cycled towards
the site gate.

'I'm going fishing tomorrow,' John
called after her. 'Want to come?'

Lisa had never been fishing, but she thought it might be better than doing nothing at her aunt's cottage. 'OK. Where shall we meet?' she shouted.

'Outside the White Hart Inn near the crossroads. Nine a.m.?'

'See you there!' Lisa waved as she turned into the lane.

The sun was low and elder trees threw long shadows across the road. 'That was quite an adventure, wasn't it?' she said to Flame.

Flame mewed agreement. He curled his front paws over the basket's rim and peered ahead, ears pricked up and fur sparkling.

At the top of the lane, Lisa paused. 'Now. Do we go right or left?'

Suddenly a dark-blue van pulled up, hooting loudly. Lisa jumped with fright. The van's broken wing mirror was only centimetres away. With a screech of tyres, the van sped off.

'Some people have no manners!' Lisa fumed, turning into Berry Road.

As she cycled towards her aunt's cottage, a niggling worry crept into her mind. It felt like she had forgotten something.

Aunt Rose's shopping!

'Oh, no!' she breathed. 'Maybe we've still got time to go to the shops.'

'We are too late.' Flame pointed a paw at the red and black VW Beetle, which was coming towards them.

Matilda drew to a halt. Lisa's aunt leaned out of the window, a furious look on her face. 'I want a word with you, young lady!' she said.

Lisa's spirits sank. 'Uh-oh,' she whispered to Flame.

Chapter
★ SEVEN ★

Lisa dragged her feet as she
followed her aunt into the cottage.
There was no way she could avoid a
lecture. Flame padded in behind
them.

Rose's cheeks were flushed with
anger. 'You've been gone for hours,
Lisa. I've been frantic, driving around
looking for you.'

'I didn't realize how late it was,' Lisa murmured, wondering what all the fuss was about. She was back now, wasn't she?

'You should have come back and told me where you were going,' Rose snapped. 'You know that I'm responsible for you while you're here. I thought you were more grown up than this.'

Lisa felt an uncomfortable twinge of guilt. 'I'm sorry, Aunt Rose. I didn't think.' She told her aunt all about almost crashing into John on Fly, then going to the travellers' site and having tea with Violet Wood.

'I'm amazed you weren't hurt when you fell off the bike. And you really should have told me first before going off with someone you've just met! But it sounds like you had a good time,' Rose said more calmly. She flopped down on to the sofa and patted the seat next to her.

Lisa sat near to her aunt and Flame curled up between them. 'John's really nice when you get to know him, Aunt Rose. He mended the buckled wheel.' Oops. She hadn't meant to mention that.

But Rose didn't seem to have noticed. She sighed and put her arm around Lisa's shoulder. 'No harm's done. So let's forget it. But promise me you'll always tell me where you're going from now on.'

'I promise,' Lisa said, making a cross-my-heart shape with one finger.

Rose smiled, her good humour
restored. She jumped up and went
towards the kitchen. 'Right, I don't
know about you, but I'm starving.
Could you bring the shopping inside,
please?'

'Um . . .' Lisa's face fell. 'Now I'm
really going to get roasted,' she
whispered to Flame.

Flame mewed and twitched his

whiskers. Lisa saw that huge silver
sparks were popping in the air around
him. The familiar warmth prickled
down her spine.

'Flame! You can't have . . . Can you?'

She dashed outside to where she had
left the bike leaning against the cottage
wall. The bike's basket was crammed
with food. There was bread, milk,
eggs and even a gooey, home-made
chocolate cake.

'Oh, you star!' Lisa swept Flame up in a huge hug. She kissed his pink nose. 'You've just saved my life!'

Flame widened his eyes. He stopped in mid-purr. 'Are you in danger, Lisa?'

'No. It's just something you say.' Lisa giggled.

Rose threw up her hands with delight when she saw the cake. 'That's my favourite!'

'My treat,' Lisa said, biting back a huge grin. She would have loved to say Flame chose it!

That evening after supper, Lisa washed the dishes without a second thought. She smiled to herself; she must be getting used to life in the countryside! Afterwards, she made a cup of coffee for her aunt and took it through to the sitting room. Flame was curled up asleep on his blanket.

'Thanks. I could get used to this,' Rose joked. 'So, what did you think of Violet Wood?'

'She's great. I loved her cara— wagon,' Lisa corrected herself. 'It was really small inside, but with a wood stove and bed and everything. Violet told us some stories about her travelling days.'

'I expect it was a wonderful life,' Rose said. 'It's a shame that some things have to change so much. Violet rules the Wood family with a rod of iron — even the men! She really must have taken to you. I've never heard of anyone from the village being invited to have tea with her.'

'Violet loved Flame too,' Lisa said.
'But not as much as I do.' She glanced
at the sleeping kitten, a warm glow
filling her chest.

Rose smiled. 'The Woods seem like a
really nice, friendly family.'

Lisa was glad her aunt approved of
John Wood and his family. 'Do you
know Mr Higgins? Violet didn't seem
to think much of him.'

Rose snorted. 'Robert Higgins isn't a nice man. You'd think twice about getting on his wrong side. He's jumped to the conclusion that the travellers have been poaching deer.'

'Violet said she told Mr Higgins that she was sure none of their men had been poaching deer, but he didn't believe her,' Lisa told her aunt. If Violet didn't think any of the Wood family had poached deer, then neither did Lisa.

She jumped up. 'I'll go and feed the animals and bed them down.' She tickled Flame gently to wake him up. 'Are you coming, Flame?'

Flame yawned and stretched. He purred eagerly and jumped down.

Rose stood up too. 'Thanks, love. I've

still got this patchwork quilt to finish. I lost a bit of time going off to look for someone who was late home,' she said with a twinkle in her eye.

In the barn, Lisa filled food dishes and water bottles and replaced soiled bedding. As she fed chopped carrots to the rabbits and guinea pigs, a thought came to her.

'Where did that magic food come from?' she asked Flame.

'I took it from the shop. Like you wanted,' Flame said. He frowned. 'Did I do wrong?'

'No. But I'd better go and pay for it. I've still got the shopping money in my pocket. We'll dash over and deliver it and I'll scribble a note to explain things.' Lisa grabbed her shoulder bag. 'Come on, Flame. Jump in. We'll only be a few minutes. There's no need to tell Rose.'

Lisa and Flame hurried across the green towards the line of shops. She pushed the envelope through the village store's letter box.

'Job done,' she said happily, patting Flame's soft fur. 'I really love having you here with me.'

'I like it too,' Flame purred contentedly from the opening of her shoulder bag.

The first stars glinted in the violet sky. A smudge of fading peach light just showed above the church spire.

'It's getting dark,' Lisa said worriedly. 'We'd better get back before Aunt

Rose finds out or she'll ground me for the rest of the holiday!'

She started jogging towards the cottage. There was a signpost beside a track she hadn't noticed before. It read 'To Lower Berry Road'.

'It must be a short cut. We'll go that way!'

On one side of the track there were open fields. Thick woods that were part of the estate Robert Higgins looked after stretched away on the other side.

Lisa had been walking for about five minutes when there was a loud bang.

'Oh!' she gasped, nearly jumping out of her skin. 'What was that?'

Flame reared up out of the shoulder

bag. The fur along his back stood on end. 'Danger!' he hissed.

Lisa's breath came faster. She saw beams of light moving through the trees. There were shouts and men moving towards her. More bangs broke the silence.

'They sound like gunshots,' Lisa said shakily. 'Come on, Flame. We're getting out of here!'

She clutched the shoulder bag in her arms so that she could run faster without jostling Flame about. She had taken a couple of steps when a dark-blue van drove up. It screeched to a halt, blocking Lisa's way. Lisa spotted the broken wing mirror.

'It's that van again!' she whispered to Flame.

The driver leaned out of the side window. He shouted to a man coming out of the trees. 'Who's that kid? Go and find out!'

Icy fear curdled Lisa's stomach. She couldn't move.

Chapter
★ EIGHT ★

A warm tingle spread over Lisa. She felt the sparks crackling in Flame's fur beneath her hand.

'You are safe,' Flame assured her softly.

A moment later a man dashed up to where Lisa was standing. He stared straight at her. 'What kid? There's no one here,' the man shouted to the van driver.

Lisa gave a shudder of relief. Flame had made her invisible!

'We must go now,' urged Flame.

Lisa didn't need telling twice. She ran past the van, where the driver was still frowning in puzzlement.

Five minutes later she emerged on to Berry Road. She could see her aunt's cottage. Running the last couple of metres, she slipped into the back garden and crept into the kitchen.

The sound of her aunt's sewing machine came from her workroom. Lisa stuck her head round the door. 'I'm going to my room now, Aunt Rose. I want to read for a while.'

Rose looked up with a smile. 'OK,
love. Thanks for seeing to the animals.
I'll look in on you before I go to bed.'

Lisa heaved a sigh of relief as she
climbed the stairs. She had only just
about stopped trembling. What had
those men in the woods been doing?
Maybe they were shooting crows or

rabbits. They had seemed really angry at being disturbed.

Thank goodness for Flame. Once again he had saved her skin!

'Have you made any plans for today?' Rose asked the following morning. Sunshine set rainbow patterns dancing from the crystal hanging in the window.

Lisa told her she was meeting John. 'We're going fishing.'

'Are you taking Flame with you?' asked Rose.

'You bet!' Lisa said. She wouldn't dream of leaving him behind. Especially after the way Flame had saved her last night.

Flame wound himself round her legs affectionately.

Rose reached down to stroke him. 'Well, have fun, you two. Be back in plenty of time for supper, OK?'

'Definitely,' Lisa promised. 'Come on, Flame, jump in.' Looping her bag on to her shoulder, she set out for the White Hart.

John and Fly were already waiting when Lisa and Flame arrived. 'The river's this way,' John said. They went past the green to a line of silvery willow trees.

The river gleamed through the swaying branches. John led the way down a grassy bank. 'Our family's got special permission to fish here. Dad helps clear waterweed away in spring.'

Flame stretched out in the grass and closed his eyes, purring contentedly. Fly, who was cropping the sweet grass, swung his head round and gave Flame a friendly snort.

'I can't get over how much Fly likes that kitten,' said John, setting out his fishing things.

Lisa smiled. 'Flame's not just any old kitten. He's really special.'

John passed Lisa a fishing rod and a small, battered tin. 'You can use my spare rod. Do you think you can bait it?'

'Sure! How hard can it be?' Lisa opened the tin. It was full of little, squirming white bodies. 'Ugh! Maggots!' she gasped.

John grinned. 'You nearly dropped the lot! What did you think was in there, breadcrumbs?'

'Something like that!' Lisa admitted,

blushing. 'I don't think I can hook one of these on.'

'Give them here. It's dead easy. I'll do it for you.' John gave her the baited rod and showed Lisa how to cast the line into the river. Lisa soon had the hang of it and they settled down to wait for a bite.

The scent of warm grass drifted on the river breeze. A moorhen picked her way through the reeds.

'You've got a bite!' John suddenly declared. He reeled in the fish and slipped it into a net in the water. 'There you go. One fat brown trout.'

'This is fun!' Lisa said. She felt proud of catching her very first fish.

John beamed at her. 'You're not bad company for a girl *and* a townie!'

'Watch it! You . . . you road rogue!' Lisa laughed.

'Road . . . what?' John asked as he fell about laughing.

'Hello there! Caught anything yet?' called a voice. Mike Sanders came along the river path, a smile on his pleasant face.

'Not again,' John groaned, but he
nodded politely.

Mike Sanders peered into the net.
'That's a fine supper for someone.'

'Yeah, it's Lisa's first ever fish,' John
said.

Mike Sanders smiled at Lisa.
'Beginner's luck, eh?' His face suddenly
turned more serious. 'Now, I don't
suppose you've heard anything about a

couple of deer that were killed last
night, John?' he asked.

John shook his head. 'Why ask me?'

'Because I reckon you've got a level
head on your shoulders. You'd know
where to come if you got wind of
anyone poaching round here, wouldn't
you?' Sanders said.

John shrugged. 'Might do. But I don't
know anything.'

'Where were they killed?' Lisa asked.

'In the woods near Lower Berry
Road,' Sanders told her. 'Quite near
where your Aunt Rose lives.' He gave
John a friendly pat on the back. 'Well –
keep your eyes peeled, lad.' He looked
back before continuing down the river
path and called over his shoulder,
'Hope the fish keep biting.'

Lisa stared after him, her thoughts whirling as she remembered the shots in the woods last night and the men with torches among the trees. Then there was the blue van, which she had seen twice now.

She had been tempted to tell Mike Sanders her suspicions, but she hadn't any proof. And she'd have to explain what she'd been doing near the woods at night. That meant risking getting into trouble again with Aunt Rose.

Were those men the deer poachers? She pressed her lips together in determination. She and Flame were going to find out.

Chapter
★ NINE ★

Lisa stared out of the cottage window as drops streamed down the glass. It had been pelting with rain all afternoon. Aunt Rose was at the village hall running a workshop on making patchwork quilts. Lisa felt restless.

Flame jumped on to the window sill. He batted at the glass, trying to catch the raindrops. Lisa laughed and dangled a piece of wool for him to catch. 'You want to go out too, don't you? I hope it stops raining before tonight.'

Flame nodded and wrinkled his little pink nose. 'I do not like wet fur.'

Lisa planned to wait until dark and then go back up to the woods and have a good look around.

Just then she heard a knock at the kitchen door. It was John on Fly.

Lisa took one look at him. 'What's wrong?' she gasped.

John was soaked to the skin. His hair was plastered flat and his face looked pale and angry. 'It's my dad. He's been taken to the police station. They think he's been poaching deer,' John told her as he tethered Fly to the back porch. He looked like he might burst into tears.

'Oh, that's awful. I'm really sorry,' Lisa
sympathized. She fetched a towel so
John could dry himself.

John shoulders slumped as he sank
into a kitchen chair. 'It's Robert
Higgins's doing. I know it is. But I
don't get it. What's he got against my
dad? He's never done anything to him.'

Lisa bit her lip, wishing she could
think of some way to help. She got

him a piece of the delicious chocolate
cake. 'Here you are.'

He cheered up a bit as he ate. 'Gran's
furious, but she's dead worried too. If
only there was something I could do.'

'Maybe there is,' Lisa said on impulse.

She told John about the gunfire and
the men she'd seen in the woods. 'And
I've seen that blue van twice. I know it
was the same one because of the
broken wing mirror.'

John jumped to his feet and paced
round the kitchen. 'It must have been
the poachers! Deer are big animals.
You'd need a van to take them away.
Maybe we should go and tell Mike
Sanders.'

'I thought of that already. But we
haven't any proof. Shouldn't we wait

until we're sure about this?' Lisa reasoned.

John gnawed at his lip. 'You're right. And if the police start going round asking loads of questions, the poachers will go into hiding. That leaves my dad as chief suspect. But how do we get proof?'

'I've got an idea . . .' Lisa began telling him about her plan to go to the woods after dark.

John listened in silence, then a wide grin spread across his face. 'What time do we meet?'

'We?' Lisa grinned back. 'I hoped you might say that!'

'You don't think I'd let you have all the fun, do you?' John said. He got up and went towards the garden to untie Fly.

Lisa was relieved. It had been really scary up at those dark woods.

'All right,' she said. 'I'll meet you at midnight on the back path to the woods. Don't do anything before I get there, OK?'

'Who, me?' John flashed her one of his cheeky grins. He jumped up on to

Fly's back and urged the pony forward.
'See you tonight,' he called over his
shoulder.

The bedroom was dark except for the
digital display of her bedside clock.
Lisa jolted awake. Flame was licking
her chin. His whiskers tickled her
nose.

'Thanks for waking me!' She yawned
and rubbed her eyes.

'You are welcome,' Flame purred, his
fur twinkling in the darkness.

It was a quarter to midnight. No
time to waste. Lisa was fully clothed
beneath the duvet. Reaching for her
bag and a disposable camera, she and
Flame crept downstairs and out of the
house.

The moon sailed overhead, as bright
as a beacon. Lisa's eyes soon adjusted as
she made her way to the woods. Flame
trotted beside her. With his cat night
sight he moved as easily as in daylight.

'This is the path,' Lisa whispered,
pointing ahead. 'But look! The blue
van's parked near those bushes.'

Lisa's heart pounded as she and
Flame crept forward. She scanned the

path and clusters of trees, looking for John. But there was no sign of him.

Flame pricked up his ears. 'There are men in this wood.'

A moment later, Lisa heard voices shouting. 'Get him! He knows who we are!'

Shadowy shapes crashed through the trees. Someone shoved branches aside and rushed towards Lisa, gasping for breath. For an instant a slim, scared figure was caught in a beam of torchlight.

Lisa's eyes opened wide with shock. 'It's John!'

Chapter
★ TEN ★

Almost at once Lisa felt the familiar
tingly warmth down her spine. Silver
sparks crackled in Flame's fur and his
whiskers glittered in the dark.

'No one can see you, Lisa,' Flame
explained softly. He hung back, melting
into the deep shadows. 'Save John.'

Lisa let out a sigh of relief. Flame
had made her invisible again!

John stumbled out of a thicket right beside her. Leaning against a big oak he doubled over, clutching a stitch in his side. Lisa could hear the men coming closer. They would catch John at any moment. She had to distract them somehow.

Lisa started to run, her heart pounding. Her whole body began to tingle. A rush of heat swept through

her. She felt her muscles bunch as she
made a huge leap forward — and
bounded along on all fours. Strong,
tireless legs carried her on. Her hands
and feet had become spread pads,
which gripped the leaf litter with sharp
claws.

She was a huge cat! A huge *invisible*
cat!

Night smells flowed over her. The
forest came alive. She could see every
leaf and blade of grass and hear every
tiny movement. The men seemed to
move in slow motion. Their breath
sounded like rushing water and their
footsteps were as loud as drumbeats.

Lisa rushed up behind the first man
and slammed into the back of his legs.
He yelled with fright as his knees

buckled. In a swift movement, Lisa changed direction and launched herself at another man.

'Oof!' The second man fell sideways into a clump of bracken.

'Grrr!' Lisa growled with triumph. She tripped up the third man who went over in a jumble of arms and legs.

The three men picked themselves up. They looked round nervously. 'There's something weird in here!' one said.

Lisa grinned. She crept up close behind them and opened her mouth wide. 'Grrr-owl!!' she roared.

'What's that?'

'I don't know, but I'm out of here!' one of them cried. 'Get back to the van!'

Lisa knew that John was safe for the moment. Time to get the evidence they needed.

She bounded swiftly towards the parked van and reached it ahead of the men. The back door was ajar. Her cat senses caught the smell of death. Two deer lay in the back of the van. Lisa jumped inside, already fumbling for her camera. Her fingers closed around it.

Fingers? She wasn't a cat any more! Flame's spell must have worn off. Did that mean that the men could see her now?

There was no time to think. Aiming the camera, she took a photo of the dead deer. Suddenly, the back door was wrenched open behind her. But Lisa was ready. She stuck the camera in the men's faces. Flash! Flash! She took their photos.

'Wassat?' one yelled, covering his face with his hand.

'I can't see. I'm blinded,' moaned another, hopping about and bumping into his friends.

Lisa leapt out and dashed behind a tree. Moments later, the engine fired up and the van sped off up the track.

Lisa leaned against the tree and gave a nervous shaky laugh. Wow! That was close. She had loved being a cat! She couldn't wait to talk to Flame all about it.

She glanced around for him. Where was he? He usually kept close beside her. As she made her way back towards the track, she called softly, 'Flame. Where are you?'

'I am here,' came a tiny whimper. Flame crawled out from beneath some bracken. His eyes were wide with alarm.

Lisa picked him up. 'Oh, you're trembling.' She stroked his head and gave him a cuddle. 'Don't be scared for me. Your magic was brilliant! Those horrible men have gone now.'

But Flame nestled closer, his tiny heart beating fast. Lisa felt a stir of unease as he gave another little whimper.

Just then John ran up to her. 'Lisa? Where have you been? You've missed all the fun!' he panted. 'I know who the poachers are!'

Lisa gently tucked Flame into her shoulder bag. He would be warm and safe in there. 'Did you get a good look at them?' she asked.

John's face was white, except for a smudge of dirt on his cheek. He nodded. 'Two of them are friends of Higgins's! He must be in on it. No wonder he's trying to blame my dad. They tried to catch me, but I lost them in the woods.'

'I'm just glad you're safe,' Lisa said, relieved that they were both OK.

John frowned. 'I might be safe, but I still haven't got any proof. It's my word against theirs.'

Lisa felt in her pocket for the camera. She imagined the look on John's face when he found out she had taken photos. But her fingers closed on nothing but empty space.

Oh, no! The camera wasn't there. She must have dropped it in the woods!

'Photos? How did you get photos? You've only just got here, haven't you?' John frowned at Lisa in puzzlement when she had explained.

Lisa thought quickly. She couldn't let John know about Flame's magic. 'I saw

the blue van on my way to meet you.
No one was about. So I risked taking
some photos. But I nearly got caught
when they came back!'

John looked impressed. He whistled
through his teeth. 'Those photos will
prove my dad had nothing to do with
poaching deer. We really need to find
that camera. I'll look over where the
van was parked.'

'OK. I'll look over here.' Lisa went a
little way into the woods. Opening her
shoulder bag, she whispered to Flame,
'Can you help me find the camera,
please? I have to be getting back. Aunt
Rose will be furious if she finds out
I've sneaked out here at this time of
night!'

Flame was curled into a tight ball in

one corner. He lifted his head and gazed at her with fearful eyes. 'I must hide. My enemies are close. Uncle Ebony's spies are almost here,' he mewed.

'Oh, no!' Lisa's chest constricted. No wonder Flame was acting strangely. He was in terrible danger.

Chapter
★ ELEVEN ★

'You have to leave here, Flame! Now!'
Lisa urged in a shaky voice. Tears
pricked her eyes. The thought of her
friend leaving was heartbreaking. But
Flame's life was in danger and she
knew he must go.

Flame shook his head. His eyes were
dull and his fur was flat. 'I am too
weak. I need strong magic to find a

new place to hide soon. But not now,' he told her in a small voice.

Lisa gulped back tears. She was secretly relieved that they could be together a little longer but she was still worried for his safety. She stroked his little velvety ears. 'Please be careful, Flame. I couldn't bear it if they found you.'

Turning his head, Flame touched the tip of Lisa's index finger with his nose. 'You must find the camera.'

Lisa's finger felt warm and tingly and the end began glowing softly. She understood what she must do.

Flame's head drooped and he curled back into a tight ball. Lisa saw with dismay that only two or three little silver sparkles glinted in his fur.

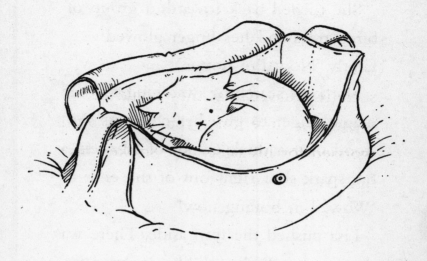

There was no time to waste. Lisa clutched her shoulder bag to her side and began searching for the camera, using her glowing finger as a guide. She scrabbled leaf mould aside and poked under fallen twigs. As she moved towards a tuft of grass, her finger stopped glowing. 'I must be getting cold.'

She turned back towards a group of birch trees and her finger glowed faintly. 'Now I'm hotter.'

She kept searching, watching for her magic finger to give her clues. As she stood over a thick clump of bracken, a big spark shot right out of the end. 'Wow! I'm boiling now!'

Lisa pushed the fern aside. There was the camera. 'Brilliant!' She scooped it up and went to find John.

John was searching the long grass beside the path. He straightened up when he saw Lisa waving the camera at him. 'You've got it? Great!' His teeth flashed in a huge grin. 'Excellent! I'll get the photos developed first thing tomorrow morning. Gran will come with me to see Mike Sanders. I should like to see anyone argue with her, once they see the photos! Thanks a million, Lisa.'

Lisa blushed. 'Glad we could help.'

'We?' John said, looking a little confused.

'Me and Flame,' Lisa said.

'Oh, yeah!' John chuckled. 'Thanks, Flame. You'd better go now. Your aunt will skin me alive if she finds you out here with me!'

Lisa smiled and waved goodbye as she hurried back to her aunt's cottage.

She didn't see the long black shadows prowling through the trees. Two large black cats appeared for an instant. One of them lifted its head, scenting the air before they both disappeared.

There came a faint echo of a

powerful voice. 'The prince is near. We are close . . .'

Lisa crept in the back door and up through the darkened cottage.

'Phew, made it,' she breathed, closing her bedroom door behind her.

Now that the excitement was over, she felt really tired. She undressed and crawled into bed. Flame jumped up and settled down beside her. He reached forward and touched her chin gently with the tip of his cold, pink nose.

'You are a good friend, Lisa,' he said with a rumbling purr. 'I will never forget you.'

A hard ball of misery lodged in her chest and her eyes filled with tears, but

she swallowed them bravely. 'Me too.
I've loved having you here, Flame. But
I know you have to leave soon.'

'Soon,' Flame agreed sadly and
snuggled up under her chin.

Moments later, Lisa fell deeply asleep.

The next day, Lisa was in the barn. She
was filling dishes with scoops of pet
food and trying not to think about
Flame leaving. She knew she should be
feeling happier – she had heard from
her aunt earlier that day that Higgins
and his friends had been arrested. But
she was just so sad at the thought of
losing Flame. Right then he was sitting
on the feed sack where she had first
discovered him, his eyes watchful and
intent. He kept lifting his head, testing

the air for his enemies' scent.

Lisa had her arms full of hay when she heard her aunt calling. 'Lisa! You've got visitors!'

She looked up to see her aunt and two other people coming into the barn.

'Mum! Dad!' she cried with delight as she ran towards them and flung herself into their arms. 'What are you doing here?'

Mrs Morgan laughed. 'We missed you. So we came back early. Rose has asked us to stop for a few days before we all go back to London.' She turned to her sister with a smile.

'You don't mind, do you, love?' asked Mr Morgan, looking a bit worried. 'I know you've probably been really bored here in the country.'

Lisa realized that she had enjoyed herself far more than she ever thought possible. And this was mainly due to Flame. She was about to reply that she'd had a fantastic time when she noticed a flash of light from near the feed sack.

'Why don't you go into the kitchen?' she said hurriedly. 'I'll finish feeding the animals, then I'll come too.'

Rose led Lisa's parents out of the barn. 'Let's leave Lisa to it. She always insists on getting her chores finished by herself. She's been a great help to me.'

'Really? That doesn't sound like the grumpy girl we dropped off at the train station last week!' Lisa's dad said with surprise.

'She certainly looks a lot happier

than I expected!' said her mum, looking slightly amazed. 'See you in a minute, love,' she called over her shoulder.

As soon as they had gone, Lisa spun round. She ran towards the back of the barn and stopped in her tracks, stunned by what she saw.

An enormous young white lion with glowing emerald eyes stood there. His fur glittered and sparkled and his whiskers glowed with light. Prince Flame was no longer disguised as a fluffy marmalade kitten. Beside him stood an older-looking grey lion, a calm expression on his wise face.

As Lisa watched, silver sparks filled the air. The two lions began to fade.

Prince Flame lifted his paw in a final wave. His mouth curved in a gentle smile.

'Be well. Be strong, Lisa,' he said in a deep growling purr.

Then he was gone.

Lisa stood there, a wave of deep sadness flowing over her. She wondered where Flame would go now to hide. Would he ever be safe from his uncle's spies? Would he one day rule his strange, magical land?

'Goodbye, Prince Flame,' Lisa whispered. 'Take care. Stay safe. I'll never forget you.'

She stood there for a moment longer, thinking of the wonderful adventure she and Flame had shared. Even though her heart was aching, she knew she wouldn't have changed a single moment.

At last she took a deep trembling breath. Her parents were waiting for her. She knew she would never tell them or anyone else about Flame. He would always be her very own magical secret. But there was still so much more to tell them. And she couldn't wait for them to meet John and Fly.

Classroom Chaos

Prologue

'Disguise yourself, Prince Flame! It isn't
safe for you to be back here. Your
uncle is close by!' Cirrus urged the
young white lion who stood beside
him in the cave behind the waterfall.

Flame's fur crackled with silver
sparks. There was a dazzling white flash
and there, in his place, now stood a
tiny, fluffy, black and white kitten.

Cirrus leaned down and brushed his old grey muzzle against the top of the kitten's fluffy head. 'You must go back to the other world, Prince Flame. But stay in this disguise. It will serve you well.'

Suddenly a menacing growl split the air.

Flame looked up at Cirrus, his emerald eyes flashing. 'Uncle Ebony rules my kingdom. One day I will return and claim my throne!' he mewed bravely.

Cirrus's worn teeth flashed in a brief smile. 'Yes, you will, my prince. But only once your powers have become stronger. Go now! Hide!'

Just as Flame scrambled behind a rock, an enormous adult lion burst

through the curtain of water. His huge
paws thudded on the wet rock.

'Cirrus! Tell me where my nephew is
hiding!' Ebony demanded.

Behind the rock, Flame's tiny body
trembled in fear.

Cirrus growled. 'Prince Flame is far
away. You will never find him!'

Ebony roared with rage. 'My spies are
looking for him. Flame cannot hide
from me forever . . .'

Behind the rock, Flame felt the
power building inside him. He let out
a tiny miaow as silver sparks ignited in
his black and white fur. The cave
began to fade, and he felt himself
falling. Falling . . .

Chapter
★ ONE ★

'Bye! See you at the end of term!' Abi West called to her parents from the upstairs window.

As the car pulled away out of Brockinghurst School's car park, Abi turned back to her new room. She felt excited but a bit nervous. It was going to seem strange to share with someone she didn't know.

'Might as well unpack,' she decided, lifting her case on to one of the beds.

There were two single beds with blue quilts and bedside cupboards. Blue checked curtains and a red rug made the room bright and cosy.

From the window, she saw that more cars were pulling into the front drive. Girls in uniform were getting out and saying goodbye to their families.

Abi had just finished piling away her clothes and books when the door crashed open with a bang.

A pretty fair-haired girl marched into the room. She scowled at Abi. 'Who are you?'

'Hi,' Abi said. 'I'm Abi West.'

'Well, you're in my room,' the girl said rudely.

'I thought I could choose any room,' Abi said. 'I've just put all my stuff away.'

The other girl put her hands on her hips. 'And I'm supposed to care? You'll just have to move it, won't you?'

Abi blinked at her, unsure what to do. The other girl looked about eleven, a year older than Abi.

'I thought it was your voice I could hear, Keera Moore,' said a calm voice from the doorway.

Abi spun round. She saw a tall woman with a pleasant face. It was Mrs York, the head teacher. There was a small, slim girl with her.

Keera changed completely. 'Oh, hello, Mrs York,' she said with a smile. 'Abi here was just saying she didn't mind moving to another room.'

'No, I wasn't!' Abi said indignantly. 'You told me this was your room. And that I had to move out!'

Keera glared at her, blue eyes flashing. 'You little sneak,' she hissed.

'That's enough, Keera,' the Head said. 'You know very well that rooms are never reserved at Brockinghurst.' She turned to Abi. 'Abi West, I want you to meet Sasha Parekh. I thought it might be a good idea for you two to share this term. You'll both have a lot in common. It's the first time either of you has been away from home.'

'Ah, diddums,' Keera sneered under her breath.

Abi smiled at Sasha, who was very pretty with dark eyes and olive skin. She wore her thick black hair in a long plait. On one cheek she had a red birthmark.

'It's really nice to meet you,' Abi said. Sasha seemed a hundred times nicer that Keera already!

'You too,' Sasha said shyly.

'I've got some animal posters to put on the wall. Would you like to help me?' Abi asked.

Sasha dark eyes lit up. 'Definitely! I love animals.'

'So do I. Especially big cats,' Abi said, warming to Sasha.

Keera pointed a finger at her open mouth and made pretend gagging sounds.

Mrs York frowned at her. 'This room seems to be taken, Keera. I suggest you try the one next door. It's identical to this one.'

'Oh, all right.' Keera rolled her eyes as she stomped outside with her case.

Mrs York turned back to Abi and
Sasha. 'I'll leave you two to settle in.
Come down to the hall when you hear
the bell. You'll meet your teachers and
collect your lesson timetables.'

'She's nice, isn't she?' Abi said to
Sasha after the Head had left.

Sasha nodded.

Suddenly a lot of banging came from
the room next door. Then a voice
complained, 'This is a grotty room!
And this school is a smelly dump! I
hate being back here!'

Sasha looked at Abi. 'Keera!' they
chorused. The two of them fell about
laughing.

'Phew! There's so much to remember,'
groaned Abi. She sat down beside

Sasha at a table in the main hall.

The room had wooden beams and walls of dark, carved wood. An enormous fireplace took up most of the end wall. The room was buzzing with girls and teachers, and everyone seemed to be talking at once.

Sasha bit her nails nervously. 'I can't remember any of the teachers' names or where the classrooms are.'

'Nor me. But I expect we'll soon get used to it,' Abi said.

'Well! If it isn't the sneak,' a voice behind her said.

Abi didn't need to turn round to know who it was. 'Hello, Keera,' she said.

Keera came up and leaned her elbows on the table. She was with two other girls. One had brown hair and freckles and the other was tall and slim with black curly hair.

Abi remembered hearing their names called out earlier that day: Marsha Clarke and Tiwa Rhames.

'Have you brought your teddies to help you sleep?' Keera said in a mocking, baby voice.

Tiwa sniggered. 'After all, we wouldn't want you to have nightmares about the ghost.'

'What ghost?' asked Abi. 'You're making it up. There's no such thing.'

Keera smirked. 'Oh, no? Haven't you heard about the Grey Lady of Brockinghurst? She haunts the school's corridors, lying in wait for snotty little first years. I'd watch out if I were you!' She turned to Marsha and Tiwa.

'Come on, let's go and see if the tuck shop's open.'

The girls nudged each other and laughed as they walked away.

Sasha glanced nervously at Abi. 'Do you think there really is a ghost?' she asked. 'Most old buildings are supposed to be haunted, aren't they?'

Abi smiled at her as she gathered up all the pages she'd been given. 'Keera was just trying to scare us. Don't look so worried.' She turned to her school bag. 'Oh, I've forgotten the folder for our next class. I think I'll just dash upstairs and get it.'

'OK. I'll wait here,' Sasha said, looking more relaxed now.

Abi found the nearest doorway and went out of the hall. Hurrying past a row of classrooms, she found a narrow stairway leading upwards. Five minutes later, after countless twists and turns, Abi stopped on a gloomy landing.

'Oh, great! I'm totally lost,' she said.

Abi looked around. Narrow windows of thick glass were set into the walls. Dust swirled in the shafts of light that managed to get through. In front of her there was an ancient door, covered with cobwebs. She pushed at it with her fingertips. It slowly creaked open.

She looked into the gloom. As her eyes adjusted to the dimness, she saw stacks of old furniture. It was just an old storeroom.

Then suddenly Abi caught something out of the corner of her eye – something pale and glowing. She gasped. It must be the Grey Lady!

Frozen to the spot, Abi gradually began to realize the glow wasn't actually human-shaped at all. But what could it be?

She crept closer into the storeroom. Something was lying across two whole chairs. Abi frowned – it looked like a sparkly furry blanket. As she took another step there came a low rumbling purr.

Abi blinked in disbelief. The 'blanket' looked like a young white lion! He was fast asleep.

She stared at the silver sparkles gleaming in the lion's fur. He looked fierce but beautiful. Abi's heart beat fast. She didn't know whether to stay or run away.

'How did a *lion* get here?' she whispered to herself.

The white lion's eyes flew open. He lifted into a crouch. The hair along his back stood up in a spiked ridge.

'Come no nearer! My teeth are sharp and my claws are strong!' he growled.

Abi almost jumped out of her skin in terror. 'You can talk!' she gasped.

Chapter
★ TWO ★

For a moment the lion just stared at Abi with its piercing emerald eyes.

Abi sensed that it was more frightened than angry. She crouched down to make herself seem smaller. 'It's OK. I won't hurt you,' she said softly.

The lion relaxed and pricked up its ears. 'I do not mean to scare you. I thought you were an enemy,' he said in a deep, velvety growl.

'What . . .? Who are you?' Abi stammered.

'Flame.' The lion dipped his head in greeting. 'Prince Flame. Heir to the Lion Throne,' he told her solemnly.

Abi dipped her head in return. It seemed the right thing to do. 'Where are you from?'

'Far away,' Flame replied with a sad look in his eyes.

Abi began to recover from her fear of Flame. She took a step forward and stretched her hand out. 'I'm Abi. This is my first term at boarding school. Is it OK if I touch you . . .?'

'Wait! Stay back!' Flame ordered.

There was a silver flash.

'Oh!' Blinded, Abi put her hands over her eyes. When she looked again, she saw that the white lion had gone. In his place stood a fluffy, black and white kitten with emerald-green eyes.

'Where's Flame?' Abi gasped.

'I am Flame,' the kitten mewed in a tiny voice. 'This is my disguise. I am in hiding. My Uncle Ebony is trying to find me. To kill me.'

'But why would your uncle want to kill you?' Abi asked.

'To steal my throne. To keep it. Can you help me, Abi?'

'Of course I will!' She leaned forward and picked up the kitten. 'You can live in my room. Just wait until Sasha sees you!'

Flame wriggled. He reached up a tiny paw and touched her chin. 'No! You can tell no one. It must be our secret,' he urged.

Abi frowned. She felt sure that Sasha could keep a secret.

'You must promise,' Flame insisted. He blinked up at her with wide, trusting eyes.

Abi felt her heart turn over. She didn't want to do anything that put him in danger. 'OK, I promise,' she agreed.

Then she had a sudden thought. Pupils weren't allowed pets. How was she going to sneak Flame into her room?

Abi tucked Flame beneath her sweater. 'Sorry. I have to do this,' she said as the kitten looked up at her indignantly. 'Don't wriggle now, OK?'

Luckily, most of the school were still in the hall. She managed to find her way to her room without being seen.

'Here we are,' she whispered, putting Flame on her bed.

Flame's eyes scanned the room and then he gave a whiskery grin. 'A safe place,' he mewed, pointing a black and white paw at the wardrobe.

'You want to go up there?' It was a good idea, Abi thought. If he slept at

the back against the wall, he'd be out
of sight of anyone unless they stood on
the bed. 'OK. I'll find something soft
to make you a cosy nest.'

As Abi began searching in a drawer,
Flame's ears pricked. He gave an
urgent little miaow. 'Abi! Someone is
coming.'

'Oh, no!' Abi whipped round.
She saw the door handle turning.

There wasn't enough time to hide Flame!

Suddenly Abi felt a strange, tingly feeling down her spine. Silver sparkles leapt from Flame's fur and his whiskers crackled. Little points of light popped in the air around him.

Something very strange was happening.

Keera stuck her head round the door. 'I thought I heard voices in here.' She looked straight at where Flame sat!

Abi's breath caught in her throat. Keera would tell the Head about Flame! Before she could say anything, Keera spoke up.

'I thought so!' Keera's mouth twisted in a triumphant grin. 'There's no one else in here! You're such a big baby,

Abi West. Wait until I tell everyone
that I caught you talking to your
imaginary friend!'

Abi looked back at the bed in
confusion. Flame sat there large as life,
but Keera couldn't see him!

She turned back to Keera. 'Tell them
what you like! See if I care,' she said.

Keera looked disappointed. She
turned on her toes and slammed the

bedroom door in a huff. Abi heard her walking down the corridor.

Flame began calmly washing his face.

'How come Keera didn't see you?' Abi asked him.

Flame rubbed a paw across his whiskers. 'Magic. I choose who sees me,' he explained.

'You mean you can make yourself invisible? That's going to make things much easier. It's always really busy in schools and as there's no pets allowed, it's probably best if you only show yourself to me. OK?' Abi grinned at Flame as he nodded that he understood. 'This is fantastic! It's going to be so much fun, having you here!'

Flame purred back, his eyes narrowing to pleased slits.

Chapter
⋆ THREE ⋆

The next few days passed by quickly.
Abi was kept busy with lessons,
making new friends and finding her
way around. She and Sasha got on
really well. She wished Flame could
show himself to Sasha too but, for
Flame's safety and the sake of the
school rules, the fewer people who
knew the better.

Flame came everywhere with her.
During lessons, he curled up on a
nearby window sill or jumped on top
of a bookcase. Abi loved having him
around. He was her special invisible
secret. It was only at night when she
lay in bed that she felt homesick.

Flame snuggled up next to her. Abi
cuddled him and Flame closed his eyes
and purred softly. 'Are you homesick

too?' she whispered, stroking his soft fur.

'Miss good friends.' Flame nodded with a sigh.

Abi kissed the top of his head sleepily. It was comforting to hug his warm little body. 'We'll just have to look after each other.'

Abi woke one morning to find Sasha already up and dressed. 'Hurrah! It's Saturday! No lessons. A day to ourselves,' Sasha said grinning. 'What shall we do?'

Abi's hands flew to her face. 'Cripes! I almost forgot. It's netball practice! They're choosing teams today.' She jumped out of bed and began throwing her clothes on.

Flame sat on the window sill. The

morning sun made his black and white coat gleam softly.

'Do you mind if I come?' Sasha asked.

'Course I don't! But I didn't think you liked netball,' Abi said, stuffing her gym kit into her sports bag.

Sasha grinned. 'I don't! I'm rubbish at sports. But I like watching. I can be your number-one fan, if you like!' she joked.

'As if!' Abi laughed and gave her a friendly shove.

Straight after breakfast, Abi and Sasha made their way to the school gym. Flame had decided to come too. He was curled up in Abi's sports bag.

Some other girls from Abi's lessons were in the changing rooms. They called out a greeting to Abi. 'Hi!'

'Hi!' Abi answered with a smile. She changed into her kit. 'Will you be all right?' she whispered to Flame.

'I will be fine. Go and look around,' he mewed softly.

Abi ran on to the court where some girls were already practising their shooting skills. She saw Keera throw the ball straight into the net.

'Good shot,' shouted Marsha.

Sasha, who was standing on the sidelines next to Keera's other friend, Tiwa, gave Abi an enthusiastic wave.

Keera looked smug. 'In case you didn't know, I'm the school's star shooter,' she told Abi.

Miss Green, the sports teacher, blew her whistle. 'Gather together, everyone.

As you probably know, we play High Five netball. So let's divide up into squads. I want to see some team play.'

Abi put on a bib with the letters GS, for goal shooter. She really liked High Five. It meant she got a chance to play in all the different positions.

Keera and her friends put on their bibs. Tiwa said something to Keera, who gave Abi a sly look.

On the whistle, the centre passed the ball. Abi and her goal attack teammate worked to get the ball into the circle. Abi saw an opening. She spun round, aimed and scored.

'Well played, Abi!' called Sasha.

'Huh! Lucky shot,' shouted Tiwa.

Abi scored twice more. She was breathing hard when the timekeeper called first quarter, but she was eager for the next game. She loved playing with her new schoolfriends.

'Swap positions, everyone!' Miss Green called out.

Abi changed to goalkeeper and on the other team Keera was playing goal attack. She was really good. Abi had to work hard defending against her. Suddenly Keera broke free. She shot at goal. The ball bounced off the net and went over the line.

'Hard luck!' called Tiwa.

Keera's face twisted. She looked down at the floor and clenched her fists.

As Abi went after the ball, she saw Flame come bounding up the gym. He jumped on a pile of gym mats. Rolling over, he lay stretched out on his back, showing his pale tummy.

Abi couldn't help chuckling. Flame seemed to be really enjoying himself.

She came and stood behind the line, ready to throw in the ball.

'Were you laughing at me?' Keera demanded.

'No,' Abi said, puzzled.

Keera scowled. 'You'd better not be. I hardly ever miss a shot at goal.'

As Abi threw the ball, she suddenly realized that Keera had seen her laughing at Flame. She was going to have to be a lot more careful at keeping him secret.

Moments later, Keera caught a low pass from Marsha. Abi was marking her closely. As Keera twisted round, she seemed to slip. Her elbow shot out and jabbed into Abi's ribs.

'Oh!' Winded, Abi doubled up in pain.

'Foul! She did that on purpose!' Sasha yelled, forgetting to be shy. Her long plait swung about as she jumped up and down in protest.

'Abi's pretending! That didn't hurt,' called Tiwa.

Abi held her side, trying to get her breath.

She heard a low growl. From the corner of her eye, she saw Flame's fur sparkle and his whiskers crackle with electricity. A warm tingling flowed down her spine.

'Uh-oh,' breathed Abi. 'Now what?'

Keera aimed the ball at the net, gathered herself to jump, then sprang into the air. She threw the ball. Up it went, higher and higher. 'Oo-er!' she cried as the ball whizzed right up to the roof beams.

Abi watched in amazement as the ball turned slowly in the air and then zoomed downwards. It hit Keera on the head.

'Ow!' cried Keera. Suddenly she started to spin round. She spun faster and faster on the spot, until she was just a blur!

Chapter
★ FOUR ★

The gym erupted with laughter. Sasha laughed too, her hands over her mouth.

'Help! I can't stop!' Keera wailed, her arms waving about and her gym shoes squeaking as she pirouetted like a skater on ice.

Miss Green made a sound of impatience. 'Keera Moore! Must you always be the centre of attention?'

Abi had got her breath back now. She bit back a grin. No one else could see Flame. There he sat beneath the goalpost, blinking up at Keera. She edged towards him. 'Flame,' she gently scolded.

'She hurt you, Abi.' Flame's eyes glittered mischievously as the silver sparks made a fizzing noise around him and died down.

'I'm OK now,' Abi said. 'You can stop her spinning now.'

Flame hesitated. He pointed a paw at Keera.

Keera came to a sudden stop and stood there swaying gently. 'What happened?' she groaned.

Marsha and Tiwa ran over to help her. 'Are you all right?'

'Course I am! Get off me!' snapped
Keera, red-faced with embarrassment.

'What a show-off! I bet she feels sick
after all that spinning!' Sasha came over
to Abi.

Miss Green clapped her hands.
'Drama's over! Take a break, everyone.
Gather round. I want to talk to you.'

Abi took a cup of water from the

drinks dispenser and then went and sat near Sasha.

'Every year we pick a team captain,' Miss Green was saying. 'Brockinghurst is hosting a High Five competition at the end of term. So it's especially important that our captain is someone who inspires others to do their best . . .'

Keera looked smug. She shifted about as if ready to get up.

'. . . so I've decided that this year it'll be – Abi West!'

Keera's jaw dropped. 'But – she's only a rotten little first year!'

'Stand up, Abi,' said Miss Green, frowning at Keera. 'I was impressed by the way you played and you kept a cool head under pressure. That's the kind of captain we need.'

'Me?' Abi gasped in surprise as she rose to her feet. She felt herself blush.

'Well done, Abi,' said Miss Green with a warm smile.

Everyone, except Keera and her friends Marsha and Tiwa, clapped and cheered. Sasha shouted loudest of all.

Abi ate her lunch quickly and then hurried to her room.

Once inside, she poured some milk into a saucer. 'There you are. It's a special treat,' she told Flame.

Flame purred with pleasure. He lapped the milk with his little pink tongue. When he finished drinking, he curled up on her bed and closed his eyes. 'I am sleepy now,' he mewed softly.

Abi stroked him. 'You have a nap. I'm
going to the library. I'll see you later.'
She picked up a folder and tucked it
under her arm.

The library was quiet, so Abi had her
choice of the computers. She opened
her folder and set to work.

Sasha found her there an hour later.
'I've been looking everywhere for you.'
She peered over Abi's shoulder. Her
dark eyes opened wide. 'Schoolwork?
On a Saturday afternoon?'

Abi felt herself get hot. She hesitated,
biting her lip. 'I sometimes need to
go over things a few times before I
understand them properly,' she admitted
after a long pause. 'I bet you think I'm
stupid, don't you?'

Sasha shook her head. 'Of course I

don't! Everybody learns in different ways. Anyway, so what? You're fantastic at sports. I could help you if you like.'

'Really? That would be great!' Abi beamed at her friend. Sasha was brilliant at lessons.

They went through the lesson notes together. After another twenty minutes, Abi sat back. 'It all makes much more sense now.'

'See, you can do it,' Sasha said with a smile. 'Do you fancy walking into the village? We could spend our pocket money.'

Abi smiled. 'Sounds like fun. I'll just put my folder back in our room. Shall I meet you at the school gate?'

Sasha nodded.

As Abi hurried out of the library, she saw Marsha coming towards her. Marsha glanced at the folder under Abi's arm but said nothing.

When Abi entered her room, Flame sat up and stretched. He made a little sound of greeting.

'Hello, you.' Abi gave him a cuddle. 'Had a good sleep? I'm just going to the village with Sasha. Do you want to come?'

Flame gave an eager mew. Abi opened her bag and he jumped in.

'Comfortable?' she said, shouldering her bag. 'Let's go.'

Sasha was at the gate. She waved as Abi approached.

It was a warm afternoon. Flame stuck his head out of the bag, enjoying the view as Abi and Sasha sauntered down the road. The village was a cluster of cottages grouped near an old stone bridge that spanned the river.

'There's the newsagent's,' Abi said, walking across a green to a large, thatched cottage that stood by itself. As she and Sasha opened the shop door, a bell rang.

Abi felt Flame jump out of her school bag as he went off looking for exciting smells to explore.

'Oh, no,' Sasha whispered. 'Look who's over there.'

Abi saw Keera flipping through some magazines. Marsha and Tiwa were at the counter buying crisps and drinks.

'Just ignore them. Come on,' Abi said, walking towards a display of sweets. Sasha followed her. She picked up a bag of sherbet lemons. 'My favourites.'

Keera looked up. Abi saw her nudge

Marsha and then the three of them drifted over.

Abi's heart sank, but she looked straight at Keera.

'Well, if it isn't the cheat,' Keera jeered. She put her hands on her hips. 'Marsha saw you doing extra work. You're just trying to get ahead of everybody in class.'

'I'm not!' Abi said. 'I'm just trying to keep up.'

'Oh, yeah, sure!' Tiwa scoffed.

'Leave her alone. She doesn't have to explain herself to you,' Sasha spoke up bravely.

'Who asked you?' Marsha turned on Sasha. 'I shouldn't buy any sweets if I were you. You might get even more spots!'

Keera and Tiwa laughed.

Sasha hung her head. She put a hand up to cover the birthmark on her cheek.

Abi felt her temper rising. She leapt to her friend's defence. 'Leave her alone! She hasn't got spots. It's just a birthmark!'

Marsha jutted her head forward. 'Listen to the cheat sticking up for Spotty. 'Spo–tty! Spo–tty!' she chanted. She knocked the bag of sweets out of Sasha's hands.

'Oh!' Sasha said with dismay as the bag burst. Sweets rolled everywhere.

Abi saw a flash of sparks as Flame leapt on to a nearby shelf. He twitched his whiskers and a fountain of silver sparks shot towards Marsha.

Abi felt her backbone start to prickle. 'Uh-oh . . . now what?' she said under her breath.

There was a horrible squelching noise. First one purple blob appeared on Marsha's cheek, then another. Big blotches began popping out all over Marsha's face!

Chapter
★ FIVE ★

Keera and Tiwa gaped at Marsha in horror.

'What's wrong with your face?' Tiwa said.

'What do you mean?' Marsha went and peered at herself in the glass window. Her face was completely purple and her nose looked all lumpy, like a blackberry. 'Aargh! What's happened to me?' she wailed.

'It's probably the Black Death. Stay away from me!' Keera said.

'Oo-er! It might be catching!' Tiwa backed away.

Marsha burst into tears.

Abi even felt a bit sorry for her. She grasped Sasha's arm and hurried towards the counter. 'Quick! Let's pay for our sweets and go!'

Marsha had clapped her hands to her

face. Moaning, she stumbled past the counter and tried to open the door with her elbow.

'Are you all right, dear?' The shopkeeper looked at her with concern.

'Mnnnff,' mumbled Marsha, pulling her school sweater over her head.

Keera and Tiwa dashed for the door. Abi saw Keera grab some bags of sweets from the counter while the shopkeeper wasn't looking.

Outside the shop, Abi told Sasha what she had seen. 'Keera stole them! I saw her shove them in her bag!'

'That's awful. Keera gets loads of pocket money. She was bragging about it at lunch. Those three are so mean.' Sasha looked towards Keera and Tiwa who were running down the road.

Marsha was walking more slowly, trying to keep her face covered. 'It's weird what happened to Marsha, isn't it?' She grinned. 'But it serves her right!'

Abi nodded and grinned back. 'Yes! But I bet it won't last long. It's probably just an allergy or something.'

Sasha still looked puzzled. 'Some strange things have been happening at school lately, haven't they?'

'Mmm,' Abi said, looking away.

Suddenly they both heard some shouting. It was coming from near the river. A group of boys were pointing up at a tree. Two of them were nudging each other and laughing. One of them, the biggest, who looked about thirteen, was collecting stones.

'What are they doing?' Abi said.

Sasha shaded her eyes and looked into the tree. 'Oh, no! There's a black and white kitten up there.'

Abi's heart lurched in her chest. It was Flame!

She realized that Flame must have slipped out of the shop and gone exploring. Climbing the tree had been so exciting that he'd forgotten to stay invisible. Now everyone could see him, so he couldn't do any magic to save himself!

Just then Flame slipped. Abi heard him give a yowl of terror as he only just managed to catch on with his paws to a slim branch hanging out over the river. He clung on desperately, his back legs dangling in the air.

'He's going to fall!' Abi gasped.

Leaping forward, she raced towards the boys.

The tough-looking boy had sorted out a stone. He drew his arm back and took aim.

'No!' Abi screamed.

She rushed up and shoved the tough-looking boy hard in the chest. He was so surprised that he backed off in amazement.

Abi stood beneath the branch, arms outstretched over the river. She was only just in time.

Flame gave a howl and fell out of the tree. Abi caught him, hardly noticing as his sharp claws raked her hands and arms.

'I've got you, Flame. You're safe,' she whispered. She cradled his trembling body.

The tough boy had recovered from his surprise and his face darkened with anger. 'Hey, you!' he shouted at Abi.

'Get her, Craig!' one of the other boys called.

Abi realized that Craig was much bigger than her. She glanced at Sasha, who had just reached the tree. 'Run!' she yelled.

Sasha didn't need telling twice. She and Abi tore off down the road. Flame nestled against Abi, shivering with fright.

The boys ran after them.

'Look!' Sasha pointed across a field. 'That's the back of our school. It must be a short cut!'

Abi spotted a stile. 'Over here!' she urged.

She and Sasha climbed up and jumped into the field. Breathing hard, they pounded across the grass. Abi ran as fast as she could, but holding Flame slowed her down. She chanced a look over her shoulder.

Craig was gaining on her!

Sasha reached the gates. She dragged them open and raced towards

the school. 'We'll be OK now!'
she called over her shoulder to
Abi.

Abi had one foot inside the gates.
Suddenly she was jerked to a halt.

Craig had grabbed her arm!

Abi struggled to pull free. She
couldn't push Craig away or she might
drop Flame.

Craig's fingers dug into her arm.
'Give me that kitten!' he said through
gritted teeth.

'No!' Abi winced, her heart
pounding. She curled her arms round
Flame and struggled to get away, but
Craig was too strong.

Flame gave a tiny mew and a couple
of silver sparks shot out of his fur. Abi
felt a weak tingle up her spine. Flame

was feeling better and trying to do some magic.

She gathered all her strength and gave a final wrench. Taken by surprise, Craig lost his grip. Abi made a frantic dive inside the gates.

Behind her, Craig gave a yell. 'Help! I'm stuck!'

Abi turned round. Craig's feet seemed rooted to the spot. He waggled his knees, trying to make his legs move. She watched his friends run up and grab his hands. They tried to pull Craig free, but he was stuck fast.

'You big bully!' Abi shouted to Craig as she zoomed down the school path after Sasha. She knew the spell would soon wear off.

Abi didn't look back until she was
inside the building. Half a minute later,
she collapsed against a wall and tried to
catch her breath.

'Gosh! You were brave,' Sasha puffed
beside her. 'That horrible Craig boy
was miles bigger than you!'

Abi didn't feel brave. Now that the
danger was past, her legs felt all weak
and trembling. The scratches on her

hands and arms were stinging like crazy too.

'When did you let that kitten go?' asked Sasha.

'What?' Abi realized that Flame must have made himself invisible. That meant he was feeling back to his old self. 'Oh, he jumped down back there in the field,' she said quickly. 'I bet he lives somewhere close. He'll find his way back. I'm just going up to the room. I want to wash these scratches.'

Sasha decided she was hungry and went off to beg some sandwiches from Cook. 'I'll bring some up to the room for you.'

'OK. Thanks. And could you ask her for some milk, please?' Abi began climbing the stairs.

In her room, Abi sat on her bed with
Flame in her lap. He snuggled up close.
'You saved me, Abi. Thank you. But
are you hurt?' he mewed with concern.

Abi looked at the deep scratches on
her hands. She shrugged. 'It doesn't
matter.'

Flame reached out a paw and
touched her very gently. Tiny silver
sparks, like Christmas glitter, sprinkled
her hands and arms. Abi felt them
grow warm. The pain faded. Where the
scratches had been there were now just
faint marks.

'Thank you, Flame,' she said. 'I nearly
died with fright when I saw you up
that tree!'

She bent her head and Flame
touched her chin with the tip of his

cold black nose. A warm glow settled in Abi's heart. She realized how fond she was of the magic kitten. It made her sad to think that one day he may have to leave.

Chapter
★ SIX ★

Abi and Sasha were just finishing classes
the following day when they were
called to Mrs York's office.

Keera, Tiwa and Marsha were already
there. Marsha's face had gone back to
normal.

Mrs York explained that Mrs Brown
from the newsagent's had noticed that
some sweets had gone missing. 'She's

certain it was just after the five of you left her shop yesterday afternoon. Have you anything to say?' she asked.

'It's nothing to do with me,' Keera said promptly.

Abi's eyes widened. She looked across at Sasha, but by silent agreement neither of them spoke. Abi didn't want to tell tales on anyone, even if it was Keera and her horrible friends. Sasha obviously thought the same way.

Tiwa and Marsha were also silent.

Mrs York looked angry and disappointed. 'I'm going to give the person responsible a chance to own up. You have until tomorrow morning. After that, I shall take steps to find the truth.'

In the corridor outside, Keera
smirked at Abi and Sasha. She went off
with her friends. They heard them
laughing together.

Sasha clenched her fists. 'Ooh!
They make me so mad!' she said. 'I
really feel like going back and telling
the Head that Keera took those
sweets.'

Abi frowned. 'Me too, but I'm not

going to. I hate what Keera did. But I'm not a snitch.'

'But we can't let her get away with it!' Sasha said.

'She won't. My mum says that the truth has a way of getting out,' Abi said. 'Sorry, Sasha, but I've really got to go now. It's netball practice tonight . . .'

'And you've still got that project on Ancient Egyptians to work on, right?' Sasha guessed. 'I was going to computer club, but I can go later. I'll give you a hand.'

'Thanks. You're the best friend anyone could have!' Abi linked arms with Sasha.

By the next morning, no one had owned up to stealing the sweets. Somehow the news had got out and rumours were all over the school.

'I heard that Mrs York is going to do a room search,' Sasha said to Abi when they were sitting eating lunch. 'Maybe Keera will own up before that.'

'I wouldn't hold my breath,' Abi said. 'But I think she might have a guilty conscience.'

'How do you know?' Sasha asked.

'She left netball practice early to go and see Nurse with a headache,' Abi replied.

'Did she?' Sasha looked surprised. 'I saw her and Tiwa outside our room just before you got back. She seemed OK then.'

Just as Abi was finishing her baked potato and salad, she heard someone call her name. 'Mrs York wants to see you,' a girl she had seen round school a few times told her.

Abi rose to her feet. She threw a puzzled glance at Sasha. What could the Head want with her?

'Grounded for a week! But I haven't done anything!' Abi burst out.

She stood in her room, looking with dismay at Mrs York. The head teacher held up three bags of sweets, which she had just found under Abi's bed. 'Then how do you explain these?'

'But they're not mine,' Abi insisted. 'Someone must have put them there.'

Keera! She hid the sweets under my bed, Abi thought. *That's why she left netball practice early!*

'Please. You have to believe me. I

didn't steal those sweets,' Abi said.

Mrs York shook her head. 'I'm sorry you still can't seem to tell me the truth. I expected more of you, Abi. I shall have more to say about this later.' She swept from the room.

Stung by the unfairness of it, Abi sank on to a chair. How was she going to prove her innocence?

'Caught red-handed, were you?' said a gloating voice from the doorway. 'I wouldn't be surprised if they picked someone else to be captain of the netball team now.'

Abi didn't look up. 'Just go away, Keera,' she said in a shaky voice.

Over the next week, Abi tried to throw herself into her schoolwork. But it was no use. She couldn't seem to concentrate.

'Keera's telling everyone that you're the thief. We can't let her get away with this!' Sasha fumed at the end of a maths lesson. 'I've had enough. I'm going to see Mrs York right now!'

Abi put her things back into her pencil case. 'It's too late for that. Mrs

York will just think you're sticking up for me. She'll never believe me after she found the sweets under my bed.'

'If only there was some way to *make* Keera tell the truth,' Sasha said.

An idea suddenly sprang into Abi's mind. She sat up straight. 'That's it! You're brilliant, Sasha!'

'Am I?' Sasha blinked at her.

Abi's idea was taking shape. She grinned. 'Remember that first day, how Keera tried to scare us about the school ghost?'

Sasha nodded. 'The Grey Lady.'

'Exactly!' Abi said. 'I think I might have a way to scare Keera into telling the truth. But I'll need your help.'

'Fine. Just tell me what to do,' Sasha said.

'OK. This is the plan . . .'

When Abi had finished, a slow smile spread over Sasha's face. 'I think I get the idea!

That evening, Abi rolled up her bed sheet, tucked it under her arm and set off with Flame. They made their way along the twists and turns of the old stairways, up to the dusty landing. There were the narrow windows of thick, greenish glass that Abi remembered. In front of her was the ancient wooden door.

As Abi opened it, it seemed to groan in protest. She gave a small shiver. It was even creepier up here than she remembered, especially in the fading light.

She wrapped herself in the sheet.
'OK. Do you remember what to do?'
she asked Flame.

Flame nodded and gave her a
whiskery grin. 'I am ready.'

Abi heard footsteps on the stairs.
'Quick! They're coming!'

She pushed the door so that it almost
closed. Slipping the sheet over her
head, she melted into the shadows.

Little prickles of warmth tickled her spine. Beside her, Flame began to crackle and fizz with silver sparks.

'I'm going back. We're completely lost!' Keera's sulky voice echoed in the stairwell.

'It's just up here, honest. The room's full of brilliant sports equipment,' Sasha said. 'I found it by accident. No one else knows about it.'

'OK, but you'd better be right about this,' Keera warned.

'Wait for it,' Abi whispered to Flame.

As Sasha pushed the door wide open, it gave a loud creak.

'Now!' Abi hissed.

She felt herself rising in the air. Higher and higher she floated.

'Whoo-oo-oh!' she wailed, flapping

her arms. 'Keera Moore. I know you stole those sweets,' she said in what she hoped was a ghostly voice.

'Aargh!' Keera screamed. 'Leave me alone. I'm sorry I stole them!'

'You must own up to what you did,' Abi said, sounding as spooky as she could.

'All right. Please don't haunt me, Grey Lady!' Keera pleaded.

Abi heard a scuffle and then footsteps running down the stairs. Keera had run away!

'OK, you can let me down,' she whispered to Flame. She drifted down and felt her feet touch the ground. Throwing off the sheet, she gave Flame a quick cuddle. 'That was great! Thanks, Flame.'

Flame mewed softly. 'You are welcome.'

Sasha was waiting on the landing when Abi stepped out of the dark room. She grinned broadly. 'You were brilliant! I wish you could have seen Keera's face! I thought she was going to faint with fright! Even I was scared. It looked like you really were floating.'

'It must have been a trick of the light,' Abi improvised. 'Bet you a week's pocket money that Keera's on her way to see Mrs York right now!'

Chapter
★ SEVEN ★

Abi and Sasha had a break before the
next lesson. They had taken some
drink and crisps into the school
grounds. It was a warm day and they
sat on the grass.

'I can't believe the Head let
Keera stay in the netball team,' Sasha
said. 'And she only got grounded for
a couple of days! Just because she

put on a big act and went and said sorry to Mrs Brown at the newsagent's.'

'I know. It doesn't seem fair, does it? I hate to admit it, but we'd really miss having Keera in the team. She's a really good player,' Abi said. 'Anyway, I'm just pleased that my name's cleared.'

'Me too. How's netball going?' Sasha asked.

'Really good. Miss Green's a great teacher. She makes you want to do your best,' Abi enthused. 'She says the team's starting to play together as a unit. And she thinks we've got a chance of beating the other schools in the tournament.'

'That's great,' Sasha said. 'It's not that far away, is it?'

Abi shook her head. 'No. I can't believe we're halfway through term. It's gone so quickly.'

Sasha leaned back on her elbows, enjoying the sunshine. She watched Keera, Marsha and Tiwa walk past in the distance.

Abi glanced at Flame. He was chasing a butterfly, batting at it with his front paws. It fluttered away and he rolled over and began biting his tail. She chuckled, feeling a surge of affection for him.

'What are you laughing at?' asked Sasha.

'Oh, nothing,' Abi replied.

Sometimes, she forgot that no one else could see Flame. But she never forgot how important it was to keep him a secret. Somewhere out there, fierce cats from Flame's own world were searching for him. And if they ever found him, they would kill him.

The next few weeks passed quickly. Abi hardly had time to think. She concentrated on keeping up with her schoolwork and fitting in netball practice in any spare moments, and then, one morning, she woke with a sinking feeling.

'We get our results for our schoolwork today,' she whispered to Flame while Sasha was in the shower. 'I just know I'm going to get rotten marks.'

Flame licked her hand with his rough little tongue. 'But you have worked hard,' he sympathized.

'I know. I've done loads of extra study. But I'm not sure it'll be enough.'

Flame looked up at her with big round eyes. 'I can fix this for you,' he mewed helpfully.

Abi shook her head. She tickled his ears. 'No. That would be cheating. Thanks, anyway, Flame. But I have to face up to this one myself.' She flung back the duvet and jumped out of bed. 'Come on. Let's go outside for a walk. There's plenty of time before breakfast.'

Flame jumped down eagerly.

Sunshine streamed into the room as Abi flung on her school clothes and dragged a brush through her hair. Once outside, she and Flame crossed the playing field and went towards a small wood.

Flame tore about the woodland floor, his ears laid flat to his head. He chased wind–blown leaves and snuffled up all the exciting smells in the grass.

Abi relaxed as she smiled at his antics. He loved exploring outside.

She had a sudden thought. 'Do you have trees and grass where you come from?'

'Yes. And rivers. And mountains. But no people. Just my kind,' Flame told her.

A world with only cats, Abi thought, *how strange that must be*. She would love to see it.

Flame seemed to know what she was thinking. 'Magic will take me back to my world one day. I do not know when but I do know it will only be strong enough for one,' he said sadly.

Abi felt disappointed, but she forced
a smile. 'Never mind. I don't suppose
there would be much to eat. I bet you
don't have shops!' she joked.

Flame gave her a whiskery grin. 'We
do not need shops for juicy prey!'

A piece of silvery paper blew towards
Abi. She picked it up and screwed it
into a ball and then threw it across the
grass. Flame scampered after it. He

rolled over and over, scrabbling at the paper ball with his front and back paws.

Abi laughed fondly. It was so perfect having Flame here. She didn't want anything to ever change.

Chapter
★ EIGHT ★

'Abi, come and look. It's our results!'
Sasha called Abi over to the
noticeboard outside the classroom.
They had just finished a maths lesson.

'What's it say?' Abi hardly dared
look.

'You're tenth out of the whole class.
And you got top marks for your
Ancient Egypt project,' Sasha read.

'Really? That's fantastic!' Abi's spirits soared. She felt like she could jump to the moon.

'You deserve it,' Sasha said generously.

'Thanks,' Abi said. 'But I couldn't have done it without your help. Wow! Look at your marks. You're second in the class. I bet your mum and dad will be dead proud.'

Sasha blushed, but she smiled. 'I expect they will. I'm really looking forward to seeing them for the holidays.'

Abi nodded. 'School's great, isn't it? But I miss my mum and dad too.'

'You'll see them in a few days, won't you? At the netball tournament?' Sasha reminded her.

'Oh, yes. They're coming to watch.
It's going to be great. I'm on my way
to practice now. There's only a couple
left.'

Sasha walked part of the way
with her. She stopped by an open
classroom with rows of computers.
Sasha was helping to design and
produce the programmes for the
tournament.

'See you later,' Sasha said. 'Have a good practice.'

In the gym, Miss Green chose squads for a practice match. Abi played in goal attack position and Keera was goal shooter. They worked well together on the court, feeding each other to score goals.

'Well played, you two,' Miss Green said. 'Keep up the good work.'

Abi and Keera made their way in
silence to the showers afterwards. Abi
had enjoyed the game. 'You're a really
good player, Keera,' she said a bit
reluctantly.

Keera looked surprised. 'Thanks,' she
said. There was a long pause and then
she said quietly, 'You're not bad
yourself.'

Abi blinked at her. Keera was
being almost human! Maybe she really
had learned her lesson and decided
to change. Wait until she told
Sasha!

When Abi got back to their room,
Sasha was already there.

'How was computer club?' Abi asked
brightly.

'Oh . . . er, it was OK, thanks.' Sasha

had her head down. She reached across to the bedside table for a tissue and blew her nose.

Abi could tell she had been crying. 'What's wrong?'

'I've just had a phone call from my mum and dad.' Sasha gulped back tears. 'They won't be coming home. They have an important business deal to do or something. So I have to stay at school over the holidays.'

'Oh, no. What a shame!' Abi sat down next to Sasha and put her arm round her shoulder. 'Maybe it won't be so bad. I bet there'll be other girls staying here too.'

Sasha nodded miserably. 'I know. But it won't be the same as going home, will it?'

Abi had to agree that it wouldn't.
She would hate to have to stay at
school when term ended. Poor
Sasha.

While she finished eating supper, Abi
thought about how she could cheer
Sasha up.

The dining room was full of laughter
and chatting voices. But Sasha took no
notice. She pushed her food around on

her plate. It was chocolate pudding, her favourite, but she had eaten only a spoonful.

'Do you want to walk to the village?' Abi suggested.

Sasha shook her head. 'I don't really feel like it.'

Abi tried again. She reached into her school bag. 'I've got a brilliant new wildlife magazine. You can read it first, if you like.'

Sasha shrugged, but then she took the magazine. 'OK. Thanks.'

'I'm worried about Sasha,' Abi said later to Flame. 'I really want to make her feel better, but I don't know what to do.'

Flame rubbed his head against her

chin, making little comforting noises. 'Sasha is sad. Magic cannot help her,' he mewed.

'No,' Abi agreed, stroking him gently. 'I don't suppose it can.'

She frowned, thinking hard. There had to be something she could do. Suddenly an idea came to her. 'I've got it! I know what to do to cheer her up!'

Chapter
★ NINE ★

When Abi woke the next day, she was keen to put her plan into action. She would have to speak to her mum and dad about it first, but today was the day of the tournament and they would be here soon. She couldn't wait.

Abi looked out of the window as the first coaches arrived. A banner hung

over the car park entrance. It read:
'Welcome to Brockinghurst School
Tournament.'

Abi felt really excited. The previous
afternoon, the whole school had worked
together on getting ready for the festival.
She had helped set out chairs in the
gym and pin up notices. Sasha had put
programmes on all the chairs.

Even Keera, Marsha and Tiwa did
their share.

'Those three seem really different,'
Sasha commented.

'Yes,' Abi agreed. She would have
loved to explain how Flame had
secretly helped her and Sasha to teach
them a lesson!

'Shall we go down? I'm helping with
welcoming and signing in,' Sasha said.

'I'll come down in a minute,' Abi
said. When Sasha had gone, she turned
to Flame. 'Are you coming to watch
the match?' she asked eagerly.

Flame was on her pillow. He had
curled up into a tight ball. 'I will stay
here,' he decided.

'Really? Won't you be bored?' Abi
looked at Flame in astonishment.
Usually he loved to be where any

action was. She bent down and stroked the top of his head. 'I have to go. I promised to help Miss Green set out the cones and stuff for the warm-up.'

Flame raised his head. His eyes seemed troubled. 'Be well, Abi. Be strong,' he mewed softly.

'I will be. I'm fine,' Abi said. 'Don't worry about me.'

She gave him a quick cuddle before leaving the room. He seemed in a strange mood.

Just as Abi reached the gym she spotted two familiar figures. They waved at her. 'Abi, darling!'

'Mum! Dad!' she cried, flinging herself at them for a hug. 'It's so good to see you. I have to ask you something. It's about Sasha . . .'

'Whoa there! Slow down, Abi,' Mr West said with a grin. 'Start again from the beginning.'

Abi took a deep breath and explained her idea to her mum and dad. She crossed her fingers, waiting nervously for their response.

They both smiled.

'Sounds fine to me,' said Mrs West. She glanced at her husband. 'What about you?'

'I think it's a wonderful idea!' Mr West ruffled Abi's hair.

'Yes!' Abi did a little dance of joy. 'Fantastic. Sorry. Got to go and get changed. See you later!'

Abi put on her gym kit. She was setting out cones on the courts when she spotted Sasha near the team benches.

'Sasha!' she called, hurrying over. 'I've got something to tell you. You're not staying here for the school holidays.'

Sasha looked surprised. 'I'm not?'

'No. You're coming home to stay with me. I asked Mum and Dad and they think it's a great idea. What do you think?'

A big grin spread over Sasha's face.
Her dark eyes shone. 'That's brilliant!
I'd love to come. Thanks, Abi.'

'I can't wait. We're going to have a
fantastic time!' Abi gave Sasha a hug.

Just then a voice came through the
loudspeaker. It was time for the
tournament to begin.

Chapter
★ TEN ★

As Abi fastened her bib and looked round at Keera and her other teammates, the excitement built inside her.

'Round one,' the loudspeaker announced.

As captain, Abi led her squad to the players' benches. She sat watching as the other schools' squads played. Then it was time for their game.

'Let's play ball!' Abi gave the players high fives.

'Good luck, Abi!' Sasha called from the crowd.

Abi's squad played well. They won their first match by fifteen goals to ten.

'We're through to the next round! Well done, girls,' Miss Green praised.

Their next match was more

challenging. The squad scraped through by only eighteen goals to seventeen.

The following rounds were tough, but to Abi's and everyone's delight they managed to win every game that came their way.

Abi flopped on to the team bench, red-faced and sweaty. She gulped a drink as she watched the play-off for third and fourth places.

Finally the loudspeaker rang out. 'And now, the finals for this year's inter-school tournament.'

Keera stood up. She looked across at Abi. 'We can win this,' she said.

Abi grinned. 'Let's do it!'

As Abi's squad ran on to the court, the school cheered and waved. 'Come on, Brockinghurst!'

Abi played for all she was worth. She scored four goals and Keera scored five. It was the last minute of the game. Abi jumped high at a catch, but she landed awkwardly and her foot went over the sideline.

The umpire blew her whistle. 'Penalty!'

The other squad took the throw-in. They scored a goal. It was now fourteen goals each.

Abi felt furious with herself. What a stupid mistake.

'Hard luck,' Keera said generously.

Abi threw Keera a grateful smile, but they still needed to score again to win and there were only minutes left to play.

The players regrouped. Abi caught the ball and passed to Keera.

Keera spun round and aimed, but it was a difficult angle. There was only one chance to score. Would she be able to do it?

Abi had a better shot. 'To me, Keera!' she called.

Keera looked round.

Abi held her breath. Would Keera give away her chance of a winning goal?

With only seconds to go before the whistle, Keera passed to her. Abi aimed. She scored!

The umpire blew the whistle. Abi's team had won the tournament!

Cheering broke out in the gym. 'Abi! Abi!' Abi's classmates chanted her name.

'Well played, Abi,' Keera said.

Abi smiled. 'You gave me the chance of the winning goal,' she said. She took hold of Keera's hand and held it up. 'We did it together.'

'Abi! Keera!' rang out the cheers.

Keera's cheeks went pink. She gave Abi a hug. Abi returned it, her face glowing. 'Friends?' she said.

Keera beamed at Abi. 'Don't push it!' she joked.

★

Abi lined up with Keera and the rest of the squads and Mrs York presented the certificates. Afterwards, there was a special tea on the lawn.

Abi showed her certificate to her parents.

'Well done,' Mrs West said delightedly. 'And you're doing so well in class. You seemed to have settled in here really well.'

'I wasn't sure I would at first,' Abi said. She turned and linked arms with Sasha. 'But now I love it here. And I've made some great friends.'

Sasha blushed. She grinned from ear to ear.

Suddenly amid all the celebrations, Abi felt uneasy. Something cold prickled up her spine.

She gasped.

Flame! He must be in danger.

She realized now why he had been acting strangely. She knew she had to get to Flame as soon as she could.

'I . . . I have to do something. I'll be right back!' Abi blurted out an excuse to her parents, already racing for a side door.

Somehow she knew just where Flame would be. She wove through the narrow corridors until she came to the staircase. Dashing up the stairs two at a time, she reached the landing. The dusty old door to the storeroom was wide open.

'Flame? Where are you? Are you OK?' Her eyes searched the darkness, looking for the fluffy black and white kitten.

'Abi?' came a deep velvety rumble from the shadows.

A large white lion with glowing white fur stepped forward. He smiled, showing long, sharp teeth.

'Prince Flame!' Abi's breath caught in her throat. She had almost forgotten how startling he was in his true form. 'You're . . . leaving?' she stammered.

Flame nodded. 'Cirrus has come to help me.'

Now Abi noticed another older-looking lion. He was grey and had a kind, wise face.

'I must go now. Uncle Ebony's spies are very close,' Flame growled.

Abi dashed forward. She clung on to
Flame and buried her face in his silky
white fur. 'Take care,' she whispered.
She forced herself to let him go and
backed away.

Flame's fierce emerald eyes crinkled
in a smile. 'Abi, you are a good friend.
Farewell. I will not forget you.'

Silver sparks whirled in the air
around the two lions. The sparks spun

faster and faster, like a tornado. Flame raised a paw in a final wave. His claws glittered like crystal and then he and the older lion were gone.

Abi stared at the empty space, her heart aching.

She would miss Flame horribly, but he was safe and that was the most important thing. It had been brilliant to share her first term with the magic kitten. She would never forget all the fun they'd had. It would remain her secret, forever.

Her eyes pricked with tears, but she blinked them away. She had the holidays with Sasha to look forward to. Smiling at the thought, Abi turned and ran down the stairs.

Win a Magic Kitten goody bag!

An urgent and secret message has been left for Flame
from his own world, where his evil uncle is
still hunting for him.

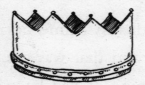

The four words from the message can be found in royal lion
crowns hidden in *A Summer Spell* and *Classroom Chaos*.
Find the hidden words and put them together to complete
the message. Send it in to us and each month we will
put every correct message in a draw and pick out one lucky
winner who will receive a purrfect Magic Kitten gift!

Send your secret message, name and address on a postcard to:
Magic Kitten Competition
Puffin Books
80 Strand
London WC2R 0RL

Hurry, Flame needs your help!

Good luck!

Visit:
penguin.co.uk/static/cs/uk/0/competition/terms.html
for full terms and conditions

puffin.co.uk

A Summer Spell
9780141320144

Classroom Chaos
9780141320151

Star Dreams
9780141320168

Double Trouble
9780141320175

Moonlight Mischief
9780141321530

A Circus Wish
9780141321547

Sparkling Steps
9780141321554

A Glittering Gallop
9780141321561

Seaside Mystery
9780141321981

Firelight Friends
9780141321998

A Shimmering Splash
9780141322001

A Puzzle of Paws
9780141322018

A Christmas Surprise
9780141323237

Picture Perfect
9780141323480

A Splash of Forever
9780141323497

More *Magic Kitten* Fun!

Magical Activity Book
978–0–141–32294–0

Sparkling Sticker Book
978–0–141–32293–3

Enter a world of purrfect Magic Kitten fun
with fabulous things to make, do and draw
– and over 100 sparkling stickers!

puffin.co.uk

Magic Puppy

BARK for joy with STORM, the magic puppy

A little puppy, a sprinkling of magic, a forever friend.

puffin.co.uk

Coming Soon

A **purrfect** gift for Christmas!